DEC   2001

# Lowell Limpett

# Also by Ward Just

NONFICTION

*To What End: Report from Vietnam*
*Military Men*

NOVELS

*A Soldier of the Revolution*
*The Congressman Who Loved Flaubert and Other Washington Stories*
*Stringer*
*Nicholson At Large*
*A Family Trust*
*Honor, Power, Riches, Fame, and the Love Of Women*
*In the City of Fear*
*The American Blues*
*The American Ambassador*
*Jack Gance*
*Twenty-One: Selected Stories*
*The Translator*
*Ambition & Love*
*Echo House*
*A Dangerous Friend*

# Lowell Limpett

*and Two Stories*

# Ward Just

BBS

PublicAffairs    New York

12432225

*Book design by Mark McGarry.*
*Set in Dante.*

Library of Congress Cataloging-in-Publication Data
Just, Ward S.
Lowell Limpett : and two stories / Ward Just. —1st ed.
p. cm.
Contents: Lowell Limpett — Wasps — Born in his Time.
ISBN 1–58648–087–1
1. Journalist—Drama I. Title.
PS3560.U75 L69 2001
812'54—dc21
2001031957

FIRST EDITION
10 9 8 7 6 5 4 3 2 1

*As always, For Sarah*

*And For Gerry Bamman and Alan Riding*

# Contents

# Sitting Down a Novelist, Getting Up a Playwright

I have never thought writing novels was hard work. Hard work was commercial fishing out of New Bedford or Gloucester or driving a sixteen-wheel truck. Novels have more to do with desire—translating desire into prose—and a temperament that accepts concentration over the long haul, meaning the ability to sit alone in one place day by day.

Writing novels bears some modest (very modest) comparison to grinding on the higher slopes of the PGA tour, magical afternoons bunkered by afternoons of routine or appalling play and reminding yourself every minute to trust your swing.

Middle-aged golfers watching the Houston Open on television in May 2000, turned their faces to the wall when forty-six-year-old Craig Stadler, playing beautifully from tee to green, missed short putts on four consecutive play-off holes to lose the match to Robert Allenby, not yet thirty. Allenby was not playing well, except on the green, where it counted.

My heart went out to Stadler, gray-haired, red-faced, so

weary and impatient, so eager to get it over with. During the four-day run of the tournament he had used up his ration of concentration. He needed a distraction, something droll or alarming, anything that would divide him from the task at hand and cause him to reflect. His five-foot putts had become a kind of tyranny. (And the five-foot putt is the golfer's equivalent of the successful sentence that completes the chapter.)

I hoped for a monstrous rainstorm so Stadler could go away, get a good night's sleep, and return the following morning. Meanwhile, Allenby, as steady as a metronome, completing his chapters with the authority and—it has to be said—the slow motion of Henry James in his late period.

For many years I have tried to find an agreeable distraction, something more sideline than hobby, some avocation that was not too difficult or tyrannical or long-term. When the sentences began to fall apart, there would be this other thing to do, my equivalent of a good night's sleep: except the sleep might last for weeks. Of course, there would be money in it, whatever it was.

I was willing to try almost anything. The truth is, I thought of this activity as a day at the racetrack. If you forgot about hunches, if you studied the form and bet every race, the odds were good that you would cash at least one ticket. Perhaps, if you were clever enough, a win ticket or even the daily double.

My children described this as Dad's search for a get-rich-quick scheme. But I only wanted to get out of the office.

For a long time I thought I could do voice-overs, the sort of thing that David McCullough does so well for *The American Experience.* I have what I have always believed was a nicely modulated baritone, perhaps riddled a little around the edges by tobacco and scotch, but inviting nonetheless. That voice, I imagined people saying, that voice has been around. I asked a friend where I might take this undiscovered talent, and after listening to a tape, she said commercials. An arthritis remedy or something to do with heartburn or anxiety. McCullough is safe, she added.

And that brings me to Paris, February 1991. A long, gray winter, the dollar falling. My wife and I had moved from one overpriced apartment to another. I had completed the novel I was working on and was unwilling to begin another right away.

The worm of avocation had begun to crawl yet again, to no positive result. I spent my time watching the Persian Gulf War on television and visiting museums, never neglecting a nourishing meal at the end of the day. It was at one of these that two German friends, a diplomat and a historian, suggested we go together to see Patrick Suskind's play *La Contrebasse*, at the Theatre des Arts-Hebertot. The author was a friend of theirs.

I very much admired his novel *Perfume*, and under normal circumstances I would have agreed at once. It's always interesting when writers change hats: poets to novelists, novelists to playwrights. But circumstances were not normal. *La Contrebasse* was in French, and I did not speak French. My wife spoke French. She dealt with the plumbers, electricians, doctors, dentists, and *Le Monde*. I was the one who sat in cafés and listened to conversations, inventing my own translations.

Don't worry, the diplomat said. We'll translate for you.

The historian seconded the motion.

My wife insisted that I knew more French than I thought I did, and, *en tout cas*, everyone would chip in with key words and phrases.

What a pleasure for those sitting around us, I thought but did not say.

So we attended *La Contrebasse* by Patrick Suskind at the Theatre des Arts-Hebertot. It turned out to be a one-character play involving a musician and his double bass. I had matters pretty well in hand until about the fifth minute, when the narrative collapsed. I had no idea what the actor, Jacques Villeret, was saying.

I inferred that he and his double bass had an extremely complicated relationship, and that things were not going well between them. The action transpired in the musician's apartment somewhere in bohemian Paris; the Marais, perhaps, or Montparnasse.

The audience was laughing; my wife and our German friends were enthralled. So any idea of assistance with the salient words and phrases was forgotten. For me these were minutes of oceanic boredom until my mind slipped into another realm altogether. As I did in cafés, I began to supply my own translation. Just as suddenly, the musician and his double bass vanished. In their places appeared a newspaper reporter and his typewriter.

The newspaper reporter was middle-aged, as was the musician; and the typewriter was well worn and talismanic, as was the double bass. The reporter seemed to have an affectionate relationship with the machine; it was his career that was going to hell.

The set remained the same: a couch, a desk, two tables, chairs here and there, a bookcase. But Paris had become Cincinnati because in my mind's eye I saw a poster that hung on my office wall in the rue des Saints-Pères: Edward Hopper's *Street Scene, Gloucester*, Cincinnati Art Museum.

My newspaperman was fifty-nine. He was a soloist, a little scornful of the ensemble. Along the way he managed to win a Pulitzer Prize, a badge he thought was not entirely deserved. When the curtain rose, Act I, Scene 1, he erupted on the stage in a fury, as Jacques Villeret had done.

I have no idea of the cause of the musician's agitation, but the newspaperman was returning from the funeral of a colleague, with the justified suspicion that his editor wanted to fire him. If my newsman had thought of himself as a musician, he would have chosen Bach, for the measured cadence and formality of expression. But since he though of himself as an artist, he believed that on his best days he captured something of Hopper. His editor preferred Roy Lichtenstein, so my man was headed for the shelf.

How did it go? my wife asked when *La Contrebasse* was over.

Wonderful, I said.

She looked at me with astonishment.

You understood it?

Everything, I said. Nothing.

*Lowell Limpett* took four days to write. Really, all I had to do was transcribe what I had written in my head during the ninety-minute reverie in the Theatre des Arts-Hebertot. I had been given a free bet at the track, so the writing was a lark, as if I had decided to compose a long letter to a friend or a bedtime story for my grandchildren.

I put into it all I had ever known or heard about newspaper reporters reaching the end of their one-way street, all seen through the lens of my own newspaper experience of decades before; alternative histories, as someone called it. My character was more restrained that Patrick Suskind's, at least as Jacques

Villeret played him. But his double bass and my typewriter were brothers, and I can remember now the unfathomable rapid-fire French mutating into measured American idiom, and my surprise when the curtain fell and the audience broke into applause.

I wrote the play, had a good laugh, and thought that I had found my sideline, except that I had no expectation that anyone would want to risk a production. So it was a pro bono sideline, with some vanity thrown in.

*Lowell Limpett* had its debut in Paris in March 1991: a living room full of invited guests; many, many drinks before the curtain rose; Alan Riding, a reporter for the *New York Times*, in the title role. Somewhere a videotape survives, but owing to inattention or too much Bordeaux or mechanical failure, the tape is without sound. Since virtually everyone in attendance was connected to the news business, there was high hilarity. Everyone thought it had commercial possibilities. What a vehicle! And so funny!

That summer I sent it around, first to friends in the theater business, then to friends of the friends, finally to the theater companies. But you know this story. This is an old story without possibilities, because all unhappy theater stories are alike. Each happy theater story is happy in its own way. I put *Lowell Limpett* into the discard file and forgot about it, reminded only when I glanced at Hopper's picture on my office wall.

And there matters stood for eight years. My wife and I returned to New England. I published four novels, did a voice-over, continued my struggles with golf; searching always for an agreeable sideline.

Then one fine day I got a call from the playwright Michael Weller. He had seen the manuscript of *Lowell Limpett* in 1991 and liked it, and now he proposed that I sign up with the mentor program for emerging playwrights at the Cherry Lane Alternative Theater in Manhattan. You get a mentor to smooth the rough edges and the promise of a ten-day run at the Cherry Lane Alternative.

If I had any doubts—and what doubts were there to have?—they were forgotten when I learned the identity of my mentor. Wendy Wasserstein owns a Pulitzer Prize, just like Lowell Limpett. Unlike Lowell Limpett, she's young enough to be my daughter.

Mentee, she said, and began to cackle.

What can I expect? I asked.

This is a get-rich-quick-scheme, she said, and laughed and laughed.


Lowell had his ten days of fame at the Cherry Lane Alternative in Greenwich Village, a slow start but full houses the last few days of the run. I was present opening night and the next night and then went home. For me, the experience was the reverse of *La Contrebasse*. I knew the lines as well as that fine actor, Gerry Bamman, did. But it was disorienting for me to watch Gerry act, and the audience react. A novel or short story is read in private, and the reaction is private; it is as private as the writing was, an unmediated experience, only the writer and the lines on the page. By contrast, the theater's a circus, the actor, the set, the lighting, the audience, and it's likely to be a different experience night to night. Still, it is unsettling when the audience does not laugh when it should. Specifically, the line "Reporters are like Germans, they are either at your feet or at your throat," yielded few smiles—and that was a line I liked so well I pirated it from a novella I had written fifteen years before. (*Honor, Power, Riches, Fame, and the Love of Women.*)

Gerry Bamman was blunt.

They don't like it, Ward. They don't smile. They don't laugh.

Do they think I'm being disrespectful to Germans?

I don't know what they think except they don't think it's funny.

All right, then, I said. Cut the damn thing.

Thank you, he said. I will.

Yet this is also true. When everything is working right, a hush settles over the theater. It is the hush of the graveyard, a palpable hush, a hush that raises the hair on your neck. There is nothing quite like it, not even the occasional a-giant-walks-among-us review you get in the book section of the newspaper, or the warm letter from a reader you have never met. This happens in front of your own eyes, and you do not look around you to judge the expressions on the faces of the audience, because you are as taken with the moment as they are. In that moment, you have willingly surrendered your identity and become just another fanny in the seat, enthralled by the actor's art.

*Lowell Limpett* is backed by a story and a novella, both written in the early nineteen-seventies. *Wasps* was written in Warren, Vermont, and *Born in His Time* in Washington, D.C. I have nothing to add to the words on the page. Enjoy them in the privacy of your own home, airplane, train, bus, or beach.

West Tisbury, Massachusetts

# Lowell Limpett

## A Play in One Act and Two Scenes

SCENE ONE

*The time is the anonymous year 1995.*

*A bachelor's apartment in a slow part of town in an American metropolis, probably Cincinnati. One wall of books, another of windows (revealing pale blue sky, darkening as the action proceeds), a third containing various framed items: front pages of newspapers, editorial cartoons, documents, and a poster of Edward Hopper's* Street Scene, Gloucester. *It is the New York Graphic Society poster that reads,*

Edward Hopper / American Realism
Cincinnati Art Museum

*The book wall has one shelf containing a stereo. This is a comfortable room in modest disarray: a long couch covered in brown corduroy, two easy chairs, a round dining room table with six ladderback chairs, and a coffee table with a photograph in a silver frame, its back*

I

*to us. The colors are gray, brown, beige. Stage center, prominently, is a desk with an old-fashioned manual typewriter, a Swedish Facit, a ream of paper next to it. Against the wall is a word processor, covered by clear plastic; it is out of place in this room.*

LOWELL LIMPETT *enters through the front door. He is a newspaperman, dressed in a once-proud suit, overcoat, Borsalino hat; it is a formal outfit, as if he had just returned from church. His movements are slow but there's something that suggests stressed steel or barbed wire. He is fifty-nine, a little the worse for wear. He carries a small suitcase.*

*He drops his hat on the couch and takes off his overcoat. He seems at a loss and begins to prowl the apartment. He straightens the row of framed documents, hits two keys on the typewriter, looks out the window, picks up the telephone receiver, and then puts it down again. From his jacket pocket he removes a folded sheet of paper, looks at it, and puts it back. The sheet of paper, conspicuous in his pocket, will remain for the duration of the action. With a to-hell-with-it shrug, he moves to the liquor cabinet and pours Scotch into a glass; and stands with his back to the audience while he sips.*

Jesus Christ. Parasites.

The poor bastard.

I hope he wasn't listening. I think it's fair to say he wasn't.

LIMPETT *raises the glass in a silent toast and drinks.*

LIMPETT *wheels to face the audience.*

Funeral today. My dearest friend.

(*In a falsetto*) Anyone is welcome to speak.
To say a few words. Share your thoughts.
About my Victor. The late Victor.
(*In a normal voice*) She looked right at me.
Lowell? Lowell, won't you say something?
But it wasn't the time. Or the place.
(*Pats the sheet of paper in his jacket pocket*) And what I had to
say couldn't be said in that company. Anyway, I wouldn't say it.
Also—
I had a plane to catch.
I shared a seat with my managing editor.
And, unless I'm missing the signals,
(*Softly*) I think he's trying to fire me.


*The telephone rings and* LIMPETT *wheels and picks up, cradling the
phone between his shoulder and his ear, newspaper-style. He listens
for a moment, then speaks in a voice just this side of intimate.*

Yes, fine. It was a long morning, Kate. And a long afternoon
because Norman Wellbeck was on the plane. He knew Victor,
too. Trouble is, you've got to brush up on your language skills
before you talk to Mister Norman Wellbeck. He's shrinking the
newsroom. Publisher's orders. So he's offering "accelerated
retirement planning" and "stimulated second opportunities."
The son of a bitch refers to me as an "Old Great." I'm a sort of
old master who's about to be de-accessioned, and what he
wants to know is how difficult I'm going to be.
You can't just *fire* someone because you feel like doing it.
He's afraid I'll hire a mouthpiece and take him to court.

Maybe a class-action suit.

Discrimination against the ethnic-group-that-dares-not-speak-its-name.

(*Pause*)

My grandfather was German.

(*Pause*)

He wasn't a Nazi, for Crissakes. He was a Lutheran. (*Smile*) Modern Lutheran.

(*Pause*)

Wellbeck's got something up his slimy sleeve. Something new for me, one of those demand bids. Take it or leave it.

That's all I can say.

I can't talk any more.

Company's here.

And I have a piece to write.


LIMPETT *hangs up. He winks at the audience, grinning wolfishly, and steps downstage, standing thoughtfully a moment, rocking on his heels. He puts his hand affectionately on the typewriter carriage, patting it. He glances at the word processor and feigns a kick. He walks to all the framed items, pointing at the newspaper pages, long lines of gray type. They are many years old.*

A life inside the news, my friends.

Why is it any different or more interesting or consequential than a life inside—a zoo. Or a ballpark or an office in a skyscraper.

But it is, because, no doubt, once or twice in your sorry lives, *you've* been news.

A wedding notice. Or the birth of a child.

4

Or a police matter?

And of course later on, the obit. We spend our lives supplying facts for that son of a bitch in the corner cubicle, the one next to the watercooler. We don't write our obits, *he* does. That hung-over wretch too burned out to be trusted with the weather report. He's your accountant, folks. Good luck.

(*Sighs*)

(*Pointing*) That's my first big story, thirty-five years ago. Usual story of municipal corruption; it's forgotten now. Probably even the principals have forgotten it, even though it was Page One.

I began with a clean lead, and I guess I better explain what that is. No smoke in your eyes with a clean lead, you look through the words to the facts. You look through the words as you'd look through a pane of glass. Or the bars of a cage to the animals inside. And we don't use technicolor. Things are in black and white.

If a clean lead were a god, it'd be Allah, suspended always between heaven and earth.

(*Reading*) District Attorney Edward J. Hook charged yesterday that City Treasurer Otto H. Falk concealed an overdraft of $57,000 in city funds. Falk, through his lawyer, denied the charge.

(*Smiling benignly*)

That was my lead.

Two straight declarative sentences. No adjectives. No passive constructions.

Twenty-six words. No word over nine letters. Tight as a drum, built on historical principles: First the accusation, then the denial. Two sentences because they're separate events.

Nothing fancy. It's familiar.

(*Pause*)

You know what McLuhan said about newspapers. You don't read them. You step into them like a warm bath.

(*Turning to the audience, speaking loudly*)

Stay with me now. This is important.

This is the history of journalism.

It was my first day on the job! They hired me from the *Carthage Tribune*, pissant daily newspaper in my hometown. They hired me to be the second man in the city hall bureau. My first big shot job, this one, and I was going to make damned sure that the lead was clean. Crisp as a new dollar bill. I was going to wind the thing up so tight that it'd be like taking apart chain mail, anyone tried to rewrite it.

All right. Pay attention.

Story came to me because the bureau chief was sick that day. Or so he claimed. There was some doubt about it. It might have been an illness of convenience. Because, as I soon discovered, this was a story no one wanted to write. Gosh, sorry. Let this cup pass from me! Because this was a story that could put a man into the deep shit and keep him there. This was a career-threatening story.

The treasurer's wife was my publisher's niece.

Most favored niece.

That's why the story went below the fold in the first edition and in the second edition (*he taps the second framed front page*) the lead, my clean lead that to take apart would be like taking apart chain mail, was taken apart. It was taken apart by the publisher himself! And now it read,

City Treasurer Otto H. Falk today brushed aside an accusation that there was an overdraft in city accounts. The charge was made by self-styled reform District Attorney Edward J. Hook,

(*Looks up, grinning*)

who is running for re-election!

And that story went above the fold. It led the paper!

But it's a little wordy, wouldn't you say? And a little imprecise, there's no dollar sum. What happened to the $57,000? That lead's as loose as a hound dog's tongue, as LBJ used to say. And it looks like the historical principle has been reversed. First the denial, *then* the accusation. And it's thirty-one words, and I think you know where the extra five words come from. Passive constructions and slant. If that lead were a god, it'd be Jehovah. It's a terrible swift sword of a lead.

And it's unsigned. There's no by-line at all!

(*Smiles*)

So—how high were *your* expectations? How idealistic were *you* at twenty-four? I'll tell you how idealistic I was. I was heartbroken. Was this the modern world? Was it for *this* that John Milton wrote—

The Areopagitica.

(*Smiles. Long pause. Shrugs*)

Nothing happened anyway.

The treasurer said it was a misunderstanding, an accountant's error, and covered the overdraft.

The D.A. never said another word about it, and won the election. *With the support of my newspaper.* (*Huge false smile*) Goodness, there were spider's webs aplenty in our town!

And the publisher and I had a pleasant chat about the proper way to construct leads, always protecting innocent parties.

7

Always alert to the words between the lines. And always giving the benefit of the doubt to dedicated public servants of which there were far too few. Let us believe in Marshall McLuhan's warm bath!

The First Amendment does not give a man the right to cry gonorrhea in a crowded whorehouse!

We always got along, the publisher and I.

He signed the paychecks and I cashed them.

He's dead now.

(*Glances significantly at the audience*)

And we have a new publisher.

(*Smiles brightly*)

I've had other offers—bigger papers, more money—but I like it here. Mid-sized city, mid-sized paper. This is where I made my reputation, and where I am shortly to be offered accelerated retirement planning and stimulated second opportunities etcetera.

When you leave the battlefield, you shoot the wounded.

And this publisher is a marksman.

(*Pause*)

I've only worked at two of them. Two newspapers.

I'm a *reporter*.

Get it straight. Get it clean.

My long suit has always been loyalty.

And my mother was a civics teacher.

LIMPETT *is sweating heavily and turns now to remove his overcoat, throwing it next to the Borsalino on the couch. He steps to the third framed paper, and taps it with what appears to be a cigarette; except*

*the cigarette makes a click when it hits the glass. It's make of plastic,*
*a fake cigarette to satisfy his oral need.*

(*Taps*) This one. No significance at all. Nada. Nil. That's why
I like it. It's just an anonymous Page One. Year, 1977. Month,
May. Anonymous year, anonymous month, anonymous paper.
No Lowell Limpett by-line, nothing of lasting importance. The
news was faceless as an ocean that day. Congress considering
the budget. Peace talks in Cyprus. A department store fire, no
injuries. Civic leader dies at eighty-four. Weather report. The
photograph above the fold: Flames consuming a mannequin.
That Page One was like life itself. What is daily life but a series
of small gestures, wavelets on the surface of your ocean.
Things you didn't pay attention to when they were happening
and don't remember later. The day's small change. Up here
(*taps*) is the feature. We call it the "Bright." It's supposed to
make you smile. It's supposed to make you believe that things
aren't going to hell. It's about a lost child. You know the story.
A little girl gets lost at the airport. You've heard the announce-
ment over the P.A. system and never paid any attention
because she's not your kid. This one's lost for an hour before
she's reunited with Mom.

(*Pause*)

The piece is told through the eyes of the child.

(*Sighs*)

It's pretty well written, and I mean to say it's pretty well
*invented*, by a lad who went on to become a columnist, Jack
Laverty. *Laverty's Lives.*

Nice feature, no prize winner.

Know something?

Never trust a bright story.

The more colorful, the less accurate.

The more stylish, the less truthful. Really, the less *reliable*.


*The telephone rings again.* LIMPETT *does not move. After three rings it stops, and the answering machine kicks in.* LIMPETT *glares at the audience as he hears a voice filled with false bonhomie. It's a mid-Atlantic voice that perhaps owes more to Cape Cod than the Home Counties. It's the managing editor.*


VOICE:

Old Great? Norman Wellbeck. Wasn't that a good conversation we had on the airplane? There's something about attending a funeral that focuses the mind, wouldn't you say? Nothing like a death to heighten our appreciation of life! Such perilous times we live in, Old Great! Danger at every turn. But one man's danger is another man's opportunity, and that's what I'm calling about. We've got an exceptional opportunity for you, Lowell. So I hope you'll call me back, close of business today. It's today's offer, expiring close of business today. So pick up the telephone, hear? Bye now.


LIMPETT *has been listening with an attitude of sullen boredom. He turns away a moment and when he speaks next his voice is laconic.*

Asshole.

(*Brightly*) So!

Write tight. Write clean.

(*Bitterly*) And find yourself de-accessioned at fifty-nine.

I never wanted to be Van Gogh. Or Cézanne. I never claimed
Rembrandt or Vermeer. At my very best. On the very best day
I ever had. I would claim for myself something of—Edward
Hopper.

LIMPETT *raises his shoulders, considering this thought. Thinks;
lets his shoulders fall. Nodding: Yes, he's satisfied with this analogy.*

So the brightest stars in our great sky are the ones who write
loose, messy, and long.

They get the attention.

They get the salaries.

And they get the girl, too.

*For the first time* LIMPETT *takes a drink from the glass he's been
holding next to his stomach. The fake cigarette goes into his coat
pocket.*

Kate goes out with one.

Kate goes out with Jack Laverty whose column's on page
two of the newspaper, his photograph with it. *Laverty's Lives.*
You can guess what we call it around the newsroom.

But he's popular, no question. He's a winner. He's number
one in our town.

(*Pause*)

Jack's for the little guy, the eighty-year-old who needs a heart
transplant or the gay with AIDS who's being hassled by his
landlord or the woman who gets her ass pinched on the bus.
Our town's ombudsman, that's Jack. Jack cares. Jack's nimble,
Jack's quick.

Some sexual jealousy here, you're thinking.

But you would be wrong. Jack's only ten years younger than I am. Difference is, he's reinvented himself. Jack Laverty looked at his career and saw it was going no place so he decided to invent another. He invented a new style for himself, too. Lowell, Jack says, "You want to spend the rest of your life on the street, ruh-portin', go ahead. I like inside work myself. Times're different. *I will not be left behind.*" He went into the opinion business. For Jack, the facts don't speak for themselves. Jack speaks for them. The facts throw themselves on the mercy of Jack's court. And Jack decides which fact is admitted into evidence and which isn't. It's lucrative work. It's bright work.

So he reinvented himself. He's on TV. Jack has a Web site!

(*Pause*)

They're an item, Laverty and Kate.

She's a smart young woman, very pretty. She's vivacious. She has a low voice and a laugh to match. She has a talent for this business. Really, she's *good.*

They're writing a thriller together, Jack Laverty and Kate.

They have some money for it. Up Front Money, they call it.

It's about a serial killer of newspaper reporters.

You think I'm kidding? I'm not kidding.

So the cops put a policewoman into the newsroom. She's the decoy.

You can guess the rest.

(*Pause*)

They fall in love, the cop and the killer.


LIMPETT *pauses here, stretching, doing a deep knee bend.*

Damnedest thing. All you have to do is *say* it, and listen to the words. Forty-nine just sounds a hell of a lot younger than fifty-nine.

Anyway.

I've got a suspicion that the serial killer is based on me.

His name is Rotweiler. Or Lufthansa. First name, Emil.

Bachelor, lives alone. *He's trying to stop smoking!*

No sense of the future. No sense of where it's at. Eaten up by envy. Mis-ter Retro-grade.

So he starts to eliminate the competition.

Until he falls in love with the policewoman.

The authority figure. I think they call her Marlene.

(*Sings, à la Dietrich in* Blue Angel) Fall-ink in luff again!

(*Pause*)

So.

Jack and Kate want out of the newspaper business and this is their ticket.

I don't know why. It's a great business, when you're young. And they have a future in it.

But who do I sound like?

I sound like the prime minister of Ireland trying to stop the emigration of young people.

Ireland's where the future is.

Stay!

Don't abandon us for America.

That's the newspaper business now, pretty villages and rolling green fields, a picture postcard of a place. *Where nothing happens.* A few old farts in the road hauling peat in carts while the tour busses roll by with a guide to describe the natives. While the guys hauling the peat are bitching about the English, recollecting the past, and wondering when they can knock off for a pint.

Why would anyone want to *stay* in Ireland.

Why would anyone want to *stay* in the newsroom.

Perhaps because they like it there. Perhaps because it offers the opportunity to undress things, take them down to essentials. Meaning,

simply

the thrill of writing a clean lead.


LIMPETT *stands quietly a moment, sipping from his glass. Then he whirls and draws, like a Western gunfighter. A TV zapper is in his left hand and the set in the corner flares—CNN, the audio unnaturally loud.*

This is—CNN. In a moment, *Crossfire*—

LIMPETT *watches a moment, Goethe contemplating the face of Buchanan. Then he commences a little soft shoe and while he is dancing he extinguishes the television set. Silence.*

My mother wanted me to be a teacher.

She had it figured out, my highest and best use.

My mother wanted me to become a professor of literature because she knew Red Lewis.


LIMPETT *hesitates, looks quizzically at his audience.*


Sinclair Lewis.

*Main Street, Babbitt, Dodsworth.*

Winner of the Nobel Prize for Literature in 1930, first American to win it.

They'd hang him in effigy today if anyone could remember his name. Poor Red Lewis, he had a stammer and a terrible complexion. His face looked like a raspberry. And he had a little bit of a drinking problem. Married Dorothy Thompson, great foreign correspondent. Not a happy marriage either way.

My mother thought that if I became a professor I could rehabilitate Red Lewis, bring him back into the canon. I guess he'd be the token white Protestant male with the bad complexion, the stammer, and the drinking problem.

LIMPETT *gestures at a photograph on the wall, evidently a picture of his mother and Sinclair Lewis. Two people standing in front of an ancient Buick. LIMPETT looks at it this way and that, measuring, cocking an eyebrow, the way you look at a disputed old master in an art museum. Hard to know what he thinks of all this.*

(*Confidentially*) My mother was in love with Red Lewis, even though he was some years older and a very famous author. But he didn't love her back. That ever happen to you? Hell of a nasty thing when it happens; you keep trying different approaches. After a while it gets ludicrous and you give it up and try a new lead. I mean a new lead and a fresh story.

(*Pause*)

It didn't stop my mother. "Takes more than that," she said. My mother thought Red Lewis was misunderstood and undervalued. Why wasn't he in the canon along with Hemingway and Fitzgerald? My mother thought the Middle West was misunderstood generally and Red Lewis in particular.

And she selected me to put it right.

And then Red Lewis would be grateful.

And love her back.

(*Pause*)

He died in 1951, when I was a sophomore in high school.

She was devastated.

*Please*, she said.

Just do this one thing.

For me. It's the only thing I ask.

Would it cost you so much?

What else are you going to do with your life?

What are your *plans*, Lowell?


LIMPETT *has moved stage center, speaking closely and carefully. Now he cocks an eye at the audience, moves to the typewriter, shoots his cuffs, and types a blizzard of words. He looks like a man at a musical instrument. He rises heavily.*

But I hated the classroom.

I like to see things for myself.

I only believe what's in front of my eyes, and sometimes not that.

You know what we say in our business?

Your mother tells you she loves you?

Check it out.

(*Smiles, and this smile could be interpreted as—ambiguous*)

I was damned if I was going to lose my life inside Red Lewis's life.

So instead I lost it inside police stations and fire houses and courthouses and legislatures and a war zone or three. When you get inside the news, living in it the way an auditor lives inside a balance sheet, then it becomes a question of generally accepted accounting procedures.

And where they fit into the comic scheme of things.

Well, they *are* the comic scheme of things. Are they not?

And of course I have a talent.

Checking things out.

That's what I do.

I'm not saying I always like what I find, when I check things out.

I don't.

But the point isn't *liking* it. The point's *doing* it.

That's the point.


LIMPETT *sips his drink thoughtfully. He walks to the liquor cabinet. And when he speaks now, his back is to the audience. He is looking directly into the mirror above the liquor cabinet. He sees his face in the mirror.*

They've been living together now for a year.

Writing their novel.

Jack digs it. Kate thinks it's a swell arrangement.

And when there's a disagreement, she calls me. She thinks I'm sympathetic, and I am. She tells me what he's done and I say, well, sure, he's forty-*nine*. Going on fifty. What do you expect?

And Kate's mother is furious. She thinks Jack Laverty's a lowlife. She thinks her daughter is living in sin with an aging voluptuary.

Kate wanted to fix us up.

Her mother and me!

Get her off Jack's back and onto mine, so to speak.

Why not? She's about my age.

Kate said, Help me out, Lowell. Lend a hand. She's driving me nuts. But I said, Nix. Uh-uh. I told Kate that I liked younger women. I'm looking for a twenty-year-old girl with a grandfather complex, ha-ha. Women my age *know* so much. It's like going to bed with the Delphic oracle.

(*Long pause*)

Or some other side of your*self*.

And I'm not in the market right now.

I've already been married.

(*Pause*)

Don't bother to look, you won't find her picture on the wall.

Fact is, I made a mistake. And that mistake led directly to another mistake; no detours. It's the domino theory of domestic life.

I suppose she would say the same.

I'm sure she would.

But I hated it.

And I suppose she hated it, too.

(*Looks up*)

You know what we say in our business. You're not blooded until you have your divorce, your Rolex, your war wound, your drinking problem, and your Pulitzer Prize.

(*Smiles*)

Or that's what *we* used to say. Probably they say something else now, the younger ones.

I'm sure they do. But I don't know what it is. I've never asked.

LIMPETT *fills his glass with whiskey and adds ice from the bucket; takes a long swallow. He puts the glass down and removes his coat, laying it next to the overcoat and the hat on the couch. His shirt is drenched with sweat and he flaps it against his skin. He picks up the drink, sighs, and steps briskly to the stereo, punches in a tape, Brahms's double concerto, turning it low. Then he returns to the wall with the framed items, straightening one. There's a row of framed documents and he looks at them proudly and fondly, as a father might his successful children. He puts the fake cigarette in his mouth, and then takes it out and points at the first document.*

The badges of our business.

(*Taps*) The Overseas Press Club Award.

(*Taps*) The American Newspaper Guild.

(*Taps*) The Bingham.

(*Taps*) Polk Award.

(*Taps*) Polk again.

Two Polks!

(*Pause*)

(*Taps*) Pulitzer Prize.


LIMPETT *turns to face the audience. He stands a little taller. He rubs the whiskey glass against his stomach, and then points it at the audience—almost an accusation. His voice is loud now, filled with sardonic aggression.*

Well, well! I heard the little rustle out there. I said *Pulitzer Prize* and everyone sat up a little straighter. Gosh, you're thinking. I misjudged him. This isn't some hack that's grabbed my arm and is chewing my ear off. This isn't raspberry-faced Red Lewis three sheets to the wind and a way to go before he makes port.

This is somebody! Lowell Limpett won the Pulitzer Prize so I'd better pay attention, not be so quick in my judgments. Maybe there's more to Lowell Limpett than I thought.

(*Softly*) Well, no question.

It's the one with weight.

And specific gravity.

It gives you some standing in our little community, and in the wide world as well.

It goes in front of your name as long as you live.

Pulitzer Prize-winning la-di-da. Though it does not interfere with the by-line. The by-line is only that, naked and unadorned. It's pristine. It's only—you.

LIMPETT *glances back at the audience as the telephone rings three times.*

VOICE:

Old Great? Norman Wellbeck. Time's wasting and I know you're there because you've got your piece to write, and you take deadlines seriously, bless your heart. But I'd like to hear your voice. I'm more interested in your voice than the piece you're writing. And our publisher's interested, too. He's signed on. He's enthusiastic. So the piece can wait, Lowell. Fuck the piece. Call me. Or call Mr. Falk direct. We're waiting for you.

LIMPETT *makes an exasperated gesture with his glass. He listens a moment to the Brahms. Then he moves up close to his framed Pulitzer certificate, straightening it. He removes his tie and hangs it over the back of the chair, and snaps his suspenders twice.*

Otto H. Falk.

He's publisher now.

The old publisher died; niece's husband took over the paper.

The former city treasurer.

It's a family paper; any damned idiot can be publisher so long as he's family.

Except he doesn't call himself publisher. He calls himself C.E.O.

(*Long sigh*)

But he's wrong if he thinks my piece is going to wait.

Pieces don't wait.

*Publishers* wait.


LIMPETT *marches to the stereo, punches out the Brahms, punches in Fats Waller and stands listening for a moment.*

I went to a funeral this morning.

A colleague, and he was a friend, too. A close friend.

Nice guy, great reporter.

We go way back.

Died suddenly.

Not in a war zone where he's spent most of his life but at home in bed. I suppose there's symmetry in that, I mean irony. We're connoisseurs of irony, reporters of my generation. It's what comes with the facts and if it's not there you know you've got the facts wrong or there are too few of them.

(*Pause*)

Everyone came to the service in Washington. There were nine eulogies given by the senior editors and reporters from his office, and some friends who were either editors or reporters.

It was a homecoming. The eulogies if you put them together, edited, would read like one of those five-thousand-word surveys in the *New York Times*, the future of the arms trade or of immigration. Each country heard from, with its own statistics and unique insights of reliable sources.

Everyone liked Victor so the eulogies were fond.

The time Victor found himself on the wrong side of the lines during the Six Day War.

The letter he read upside down on Kurt Waldheim's desk.

The time he was mistaken for a southern governor and whisked away to a secret meeting at the 1972 Republican National Convention.

His harmless vanities: Custom-made shirts and a Gucci case for his toy.


LIMPETT *pauses, looks quizzically at the audience. Considers, explains:*

Word processor.

Portable, so you can carry it into battle. Out of battle, too.

(*Sighs*)

He had Gucci make him a case for the toy. Then someone said next time he got his teeth fixed, Gucci could make him a molar. The correspondent with Gucci *teeth*.

Well, why not?

Ted Williams had custom-made bats.

Even Jack Laverty has a—fucking Web site.

There were so many, many stories this morning.

Victor giving five hundred dollars to a colleague down on his luck. Victor falling on top of a child during a bombing raid on the Golan; and staying there until it was safe to move. Victor in Saigon, Victor in Sacramento, Victor here, Victor there, always filing, a torrent of words. Even Norman Wellbeck had a fond word. The fact that Victor never got his Pulitzer; and he was one of those who deserved one.

(*Pause*)

So many don't.

(*Smiles*)

Many of the eulogies were hilarious, and well told because journalists are excellent raconteurs. The audience laughed out loud more than once. Some of the anecdotes were the same anecdotes turned inside out, people and places and punch lines changed because of memory loss. So we would often be hearing two versions of the same song.

LIMPETT *smiles, listening to Fats Waller.*

Even his widow smiled.

I could not see his children. Perhaps they were smiling, too. No doubt they were.

Daddy had so many good, close friends.

(*Long pause*)

They kept coming to the front of the church in their dark suits, speaking their fond farewells, leaving us touched, remembering Victor. And not all the stories were sentimental because Victor was a serious reporter who had done serious work.

And I was miserable, listening to them. Not that the stories were unkind or indiscreet; they weren't. In their own exaggerated way, they were consoling. They were well told. Victor had led an exciting life and a useful one, and the eulogies were only recognizing that: The achievement. In our business. Praising Victor, they were praising *themselves*.

So the ceremony was—impious.

Perhaps that's the wrong word.

But "sacrilegious" doesn't fit, somehow.

(*Pause*)

It's the pull of this damned business. It's stronger than we are, stronger than the sum of its parts. Journalism is stronger than law or medicine, stronger than the locker room, stronger even than the army, because most soldiers live their entire lives without hearing a shot fired in anger. If you're a reporter, that's *all you are*.

If Victor were a surgeon, would his fellow doctors have lined up to speak of the superb by-pass performed in 1973? The brilliant vasectomy in '84? *I remember the time when Doctor Victor drank six martinis and performed a flawless liver transplant before collapsing into the arms of the anesthesiologist and throwing up on her shoes.*

Like hell they would. They'd talk about his gift for friendship. His many charities. They'd talk about his beautiful family. They'd talk about his golf game, maybe.

(*Pause*)

Or his financial acumen. Doctor Victor the first to incorporate himself and build a medical center on an exquisitely complex and absolutely legal sale-and-lease-back maneuver that withstood four IRS audits.

LIMPETT *sits down abruptly at the typewriter. We can hear him breathing. He unbuttons his shirt collar. He fits a sheet of white paper into the machine and sits glaring at it, a newsman about to go to work. Then he looks up, leaning forward, his chin on the type-writer carriage. He's going to try to sum things up, so he turns off the Waller.*

Listen. We're always undermining ourselves.

Sarcasm is inferior to irony.

And irony is inferior to judgment. I mean *verdict.*

(*Pause*)

My hope was that someone, anyone, would have had the decency to say how much Victor loved his wife and children. I'm sure he did. He said he did. Most of us do. Or how much he loved the beauty of things, their symmetry. The symmetry of a simple declarative sentence. That was what kept him going, not only as a reporter but as a human being. That's his horizon, the boundary between the known and the unknown.

(*Pause*)

And there is a beauty to it, this horizon-line that lies between the action and the description of the action. And *you,* who *you* are determines the bearing. You are the navigator. And it isn't done by instruments alone. And it's not *bright work.*


LIMPETT *makes a little gesture with his hand.*

I don't know how I feel about it.

I'm not Jack Laverty.

I know that somewhere inside the celebrated career was an uncelebrated man. And that the man was more important than the career but on his death day only the career mattered.

25

It was why we were there, after all. It was the career that was honored.

So Victor's memorial service was not impious or sacrilegious.

It was *mortifying*.

(*A pause, and the pause lengthens into a silence*)

But we don't do any better with our obits than we do with yours.

*The stage goes dark for thirty seconds only. After a few moments we hear the sound of typing. It is hesitant at first, then confident, gathering speed, as the lights go up full.*

SCENE TWO

LIMPETT *is at his typewriter. It is only a few moments later, but he's hard at it. He's looking at a spiral notebook and typing with great speed. When the telephone rings, he is startled and looks up; his hands fly off the keyboard. He has been in deep concentration.*
VOICE:

Bill Green, Lowell. Poker game's cancelled. I've got the gout again. My goddamned toe looks like W.C. Field's nose. We'll do it again next week, usual time, usual place.

LIMPETT *shakes his head, smiles, makes a note. And glowers when the phone rings again.*
FEMALE VOICE:

Lowell? It's Mark's birthday tomorrow. Just so you don't forget. Give him a call, please. And I don't suppose it would kill you if you sent him a check. The economy's rotten up here. I heard about Victor, Lowell, and I'm sorry. I know how close you were. *Don't forget about Mark.*

LIMPETT *rises heavily and goes to the phone and makes a note on a pad, and returns to the typewriter, trying to find his concentration. When the phone rings again, he buries his face in his hands. But when he hears who it is, he rises and commences a soft shoe, gliding to the liquor cabinet where he begins to pour himself another drink.*
KATE:

(*Laughter in her voice*) Lowell? I know what you're doing, you old fart. You're standing at the liquor cabinet, pissed because you're phone's rung. You're Jesus Christ in Gethsemane, waiting for the betrayal. Wellbeck says you won't pick up the telephone. That Lowell, he says. What a character! But what he really means is, What a pain in the ass. It'd be good, Lowell, if you weren't so *adversarial*, wearing your crown of thorns there. I wish you'd call. Lotsa rumors in the newsroom. If you'd call Wellbeck and listen to what he has to say—well then, we could put some of the worst rumors to rest. Right? Listen to this one. They're going to make you the paper's ombudsman. 'Course, half the staff would quit, that was the case. Which is maybe why they want to do it. Lowell? Please call me. Or call Wellbeck and then call me. 'Bye, darling.

LIMPETT *has listened to all this with growing alarm. He returns to his typewriter and resumes work, the typing slower now. He makes* one mistake *after another. His concentration is broken and it's obvious what broke it.*

(*Shouting*) Shit!

Ombudsman. They used to call him the *editor*. That's what he's supposed to do, check for fairness and accuracy. And if he fails at that, there are plenty of other ombudsmen to set him straight. They're called *readers*.

LIMPETT *sighs, tries another sentence, but it falls to pieces.*

I can type one hundred and thirty-five words a minute and when I was younger I could do it with a stenographer's accuracy. I like a hard action. I like the action that when you hit the key it sounds like a sharp single to right. And then you hear the applause. I like a heavy machine that won't move around on you, that won't slip or shift its ground.

Kate's given me some advice. She works on one of those (*indicates the word processor*) and thinks I ought to work on one, too, because it's so efficient and easy. Eliminates the donkey work, she says. You can edit as you go along. You can shift paragraphs. *Sentences*, even. She doesn't understand that when something's wrong with a paragraph you don't solve it by moving the paragraph. Something's wrong at the *heart*. You rewrite from the inside out, starting with the *heart*. Any good reporter knows this.

(*Pause*)

I love the newsroom, though it's sort of gotten away from me lately. I love it less than I used to. I don't know it in the way that I did. The *sound* is different, no typewriters, and the smell, too. No cigarette smoke. The newsroom is like an old friend who's had his face lifted and his hair transplanted. He's an old friend but he isn't the same any more. He works out at the gym and eats carefully. He uses slang that you don't understand. And he has some suggestions for you, too, that you don't want to hear.

Do you think you could, like, loosen up the lead a little, Lowell? Let some air in? And we're not going to cut your nuts off if you deploy an adjective from time to time.

Or an adverb.

Like, Lowell, *hello*? Do you see what I'm saying here?

We're trying to make it user-friendly. We're welcoming the reader. We're putting out our hand and saying, How-de-do! Come in and spend some time with us. We're good company. We're better company than your television set.

So it's a beauty contest. Our bimbo versus their bimbo.

(*Sighs*)

Well.

I was working on a piece when Victor died. (*Nods at his typewriter*) It's *this* piece, a profile of one of our local politicians. These pieces are then and now pieces, meaning the distance between what they believed then and what they say now. This particular politician has been a little impetuous. *Elastic?* It's no crime but it doesn't make her Thomas Jefferson either. I've written about her before and I'll write about her again. The only thing I've got to set aside is that she's a friend of Kate's. You would think that would be to my advantage, but it isn't. It isn't to my advantage at all.

The personal element.

Any way to move you around.

Forget your responsibilities.

(*Pause*)

Kate went to school with this young woman, who's now running for Congress. And it looks like she'll win, if you believe polls. She ran two years ago and damn near won but some damaging things were said that can't be unsaid, though she's trying to unsay them. Some of the material won't do her any good, as she knows, and Kate knows, too.

C'mon, Lowell. Give her a break. She's a good egg; she's on the right side of things. If you got to know her, really know her, you'd like her. You've more in common than you think. What is it you say? If you've had any kind of life you've made a mistake or two and they're not always mistakes you're proud of; but you shouldn't get your eyes clawed out for them either. Remember Herblock, the cartoonist? When Nixon won in sixty-eight, Herblock gave him a shave. He gave Richard Nixon a fresh start.

(*Pause*)

But I don't run a barber shop.

LIMPETT *moves to the typewriter and hits a key.*

Kate didn't care for that answer. It's only the latest in a series of disagreements.

She goes, God, Lowell. Why are you so irascible?

Lighten up, Lowell.

One of these days you're going to disappear inside your news.

Lighten up.

She's laughing now. She goes, "One of these days someone's going to look around the newsroom and say, 'What's happened to Lowell Limpett?' 'Oh,' I'll say, 'Didn't you hear? Lowell disappeared into the news hole. The news hole opened up and Lowell fell into it. Terrible thing. And it closed over him and now he's stuck. Poor darling.'"

Lighten up.

Lowell, darling.

LIMPETT *takes a large box from the lower shelf of the bookcase and puts it on his desk, next to the Facit typewriter. He opens it and brings out a dozen bulging manila envelopes, one by one. He arranges them clumsily on his desk.*

I do most of the telephone reporting at the office and the writing at home.

I've never missed a deadline in my life.

And I don't take six weeks to write a newspaper article. Week goes by and I'm not in the paper I begin to get nervous. I wonder if I've lost it. But you never lose it in the newspaper business because the news is always there in front of your eyes. You have to get there first, of course. You have to want to do it. When the door swings open you have to be willing to walk through it, any hour of every day. You can't say, "Sorry, boss, it's my tenth wedding anniversary tonight and my wife and I planned to go to the theater and have dinner and she's counting on it. I am, too." You have to say, "What's the address again? What happened there?"

And you go to the address, collect the news, and write about it for next day's paper. And then you forget about it because, once it's in the paper, it's *dead*. It's as dead as anything on earth. And you know one thing for damned sure. It's not *light*.

(*Indicates the Facit*)

I've had that for twenty-five years.

It's Swedish made.

Built to last, like a Volvo.

Built to write twenty-six word leads without slipping or shifting its ground.

It'll write about good eggs and it'll write about bad eggs but it doesn't give shaves.

My wife bought it for me, our tenth wedding anniversary. That was one of the ones I did not spend with her because I was writing a piece for the paper. The desk called. I was walking out the door with her, and I damn near kept on going. But I didn't. When you're a reporter, you answer the fucking telephone.

So there was no tenth anniversary dinner that night.

But we gave each other presents. She gave me the Facit and I gave her a two-volume Shakespeare. A pretty edition. She joked that while I was writing on the Facit she could be reading the sonnets. While she waited to go to the theater and dinner afterwards.

She had a good heart.

And I suppose she still does.

Despite the bitterness between us.

(*Pause*)

When our son was born I was in Vietnam.

We didn't have a regular correspondent because of the expenses. We used the wires then. The war, the biggest story in the world. They sent people out on temporary duty, six-month tours. They knew I'd get the job done. They knew they'd need their own man there, so they sent me.

You're the best we've got, Lowell. Go out there and make sense of it. *Report* it. Spare me the hearts and flowers; I get those daily delivery in the *Washington fucking Post*. Report it like you'd report a department store fire. But I don't have to tell you that, Lowell. That's what you do best. See you in October. File every day. Keep expenses down.

And I did, too.

Filed every day.

Kept expenses down.

LIMPETT *backs away from the Facit and moves to the wall containing his badges. He takes the fake cigarette out of his pocket.*

(*Taps*) Won this.

(*Taps*) Won that.

The Overseas Press Club and the Pulitzer.

Because I was damn near killed.

Ooooooo-la-la. "Damn near killed" was he? My goodness, what a man of parts is Lowell Limpett! Is there anything old Lowell hasn't done? Lowell Limpett's got everything but the Rolex!

It was thirty years ago last week.

And it's true, what they say. It moves you around.

And let me tell you something else. It makes a hell of a piece. The material's superb, and it's verified by your own eyes. (*Gestures*) It's right there in front of you, this news. But it's harder to write than you might think because the secret isn't getting yourself into it, it's keeping yourself out of it. That's the First Rule and the only one that you have to obey one hundred percent of the time, because you're the reporter. Someone else is the subject. Hard to do but not impossible. You only have to stretch things a little, in order that you don't violate the First Rule.

I wrote it in longhand in the field hospital in Nha Trang. The surgeon let me use his phone to dictate to the desk, and it cost them a fortune. I reversed the charges even though the doctor said, Forget it. Put this one on Uncle Sugar.

I said, Uh-uh.

In this business you pay your own way.

You keep expenses down, but you pay your own way.

That's Rule Two.

(*Pause*)

I was still in the hospital when Mark was born.

We're cabling back and forth, my wife and me.

She wanted to call him Lowell but I said nix.

(*Pause*)

I sort of lost it. I think it was the drugs. I was crazy. I was bawling.

I think it was the first time I'd cried since my father died.

The nurse took a look at the cable from my wife and asked me what was wrong with Lowell. Lowell Limpett, Jr., had a nice ring. Isn't he your first-born son?

(*Pause*)

I couldn't explain it. I was a mess. I only knew that Lowell was wrong, in some way that I could not define. The nurse gave me another injection and the next day we wrote a cable together, protesting Lowell. Or she wrote it. I was in no shape to write anything.

(*Almost pleading*) It took everything I had to write the I-was-there piece for the newspaper. Probably I was still living inside

*that* news. I was in pain. I was out of breath. I didn't have anything left. I'd always held something in reserve and now I had
nothing. I was frightened, alone in a strange place. I'd damn
near died.

It was too much.

The nurse kept after me, *What's wrong with Lowell?*

But the truth was, I didn't know. I broke down and I don't
know why. Was it the *fact* of him? I think in some way I was
afraid for him, as I was afraid for myself. God, it's an ugly
world. I'd been so lucky. I'd used up my ration, and who was to
say that I hadn't used his up, too? You're only given so much
and you have to use it wisely and I'd squandered mine. I'd dug
deep, although I hadn't much choice, considering the alternative.

Had to be the drugs, I said finally.

Morphine, mostly. I wasn't thinking clearly.

I was out of my head.

And much later I said, I've got it now.

It's the by-line, Lowell Limpett.

What if he wanted to go into the newspaper business?

(*Pause*)

*One Lowell Limpett in the newspaper business is enough.*

(*Pause*)

So we called him Mark. And he had no interest in reporting.
He dropped out of college and became a *farmer*. He farms a
piece of land in western Massachusetts. He does all right, too.
He says he likes the land and the pace of things in the hill
towns, and his mother lives nearby. He has a girlfriend. And
they have a child. He says he likes farming because it's solid. It's
natural. It's solid as a brick wall, he said, and of course I

respond to that. I know what he's saying. He means it's solid as a twenty-six-word lead.

LIMPETT *returns stage front, resting his hand on the Facit. He looks at the glass he's held all this time, obviously wondering whether to refill it. He wants to, but he doesn't. He takes a package of real cigarettes out of the desk drawer and looks at it; and returns it to the drawer. He puts the glass on the table.*

(*Touching the Facit*)

At first I hated it. It had a tendency to jump at slow speeds. I'd always used an Underwood, American-made. I'd used an Underwood in the way I'd always driven a Pontiac. But I switched, and now I'm glad I did. This is my final machine, unless it wears out and that's impossible. Swedes don't wear out, though sometimes they break down.

(*Coughs*)

That's what happened to me in South Vietnam.

(*Pause*)

It was dusk; the valley green with hope and happiness. As the sun retreated the valley was the color of smoke, and ahead of us a silent village, little huts surrounded by green. I thought everything in my life had brought me to this moment, with a troop of soldiers at the edge of a settlement.

The air was mild.

Someone lit a cigarette.

We heard the sound of human voices.

(*Pause*)

I was one of those born for seeing. And what I saw now was a house explode. And the people inside it, they exploded too.

The sergeant next to me fell dead. And I did not move. I did not aid the fallen sergeant. I watched the houses burn. I watched the people die. And when I, too, was on the ground I did not stop watching. And making notes, though my hand was shaking so badly those notes are unreadable today. I remembered them well enough. I had no need to consult them. The events were in my memory whole and complete. They still are. The valley at dusk, the silent village, the house exploding, the sergeant falling. My own blood: Blood on my hands, blood on my notebook. At the edge of a settlement.

It was a settlement, all right.


LIMPETT *pauses, and the pause lengthens into a silence, and when he speaks it is with fury.*

Don't give me any post-traumatic-stress-syndrome horseshit. *Please.* Don't.

Let's let one word do the work of four. I was *ashamed.*

I had blood on my hands. Lying in the hospital, lashed to the gills with morphine, I hated the name *Lowell Limpett.* Limpet. Do you know what a limpet is? A mollusk that adheres to any material that's near to hand, and never lets go. And if you *embrace* this material, finding it *symmetrical,* loving it to death— well then, they give you the Pulitzer Prize.


LIMPETT *sighs; enough of that. He gathers himself; picks up the fat folders, fanning them like an oversize deck of cards. Two or three fall to the floor. There are many, many folders.*

(*Aggressively*)

I've got every piece I've ever written.

Every one. Not on microfilm and not on some fucking floppy disk but the original piece. The thing itself. I've been in this business forty years and I've averaged close to two hundred and fifty words a day, every day. That's a conservative estimate because with these numbers you don't need to exaggerate.

Know how many words that is? It's close to three *million*. *Published*.

Published words, the news. Good news and bad.

It's hard, in these circumstances, to be *light*. As Kate would like.

Not if you're in the news hole and have trouble climbing out.

Carrying around three million words.

Wouldn't you say?

LIMPETT *replaces the folders in the box. He stoops to retrieve those on the floor and puts them in the box, too. Closes the box and lugs it back to the shelf; tucks it in. He returns to the typewriter table to fetch his glass. The sentence "it's close to three million" seems to hang in the air as* LIMPETT *swallows the whiskey.*

*The telephone rings.* LIMPETT *waits until the answering machine kicks in.*

KATE:

Some funny stuff going down, Lowell. Jack's been in Wellbeck's office for an hour and they're laughing. I don't know. Maybe they're telling jokes. But do you know something? I don't think they are. Wellbeck's got that *look*. And Jack's got a look, too. You know what they look like? They look like two guys at the roulette wheel; wondering where the ball will bounce. Lowell? Watch your back.


LIMPETT *has been listening thoughtfully. When Kate rings off, he nods as if to say—What else is new?*

My *father* was a newspaperman. Not in the newsroom or in the front office.

He was a printer. He operated a linotype, hard, dirty work. Dangerous, too. This was fifty years ago when newspapers were still using hot type. And he was fast, like me.

He was an educated man, after a fashion.

He was self-educated.

Big shots, he'd say.

(*Gesturing at the audience*)

He said what *you* say.

Reporters are like Germans.

They're either at your feet or at your throat.

Big shot reporters with their adolescent egos, swelled heads, and thin skins. He'd go, They can write all they want but they can't get it read without me. Without me, it doesn't show up in the paper. It's just words on a piece of foolscap. Words that aren't read don't mean squat and might as well not've been written. (*Pause*) He was a proud man.

Even Mister Sinclair Fucking Lewis, who your mother thinks the sun rises and sets by, isn't worth squat without the type on the page. Without a printer, he's a bum.

My father was at his machine eight hours a day, five days a

week, until he died. He had dozens of small scars on his hands and wrists, burns from the hot lead. This was at the *Carthage Tribune*.

(*Pause*)

One thing I always regretted. He never saw my Pulitzer. And I always wanted him to meet Victor. They would've liked each other, those two. They had similar takes on the world. He would have said to Victor what he said to me.

My father told me just before he died that if I ever went into this business, God forbid, that it was best to go in as a big shot, as a ruh-porter. And if I went about it correctly. Perhaps I could avoid disgrace.

(*Smiles*)

I believe that was the word he used.

It might have been cowardice. (*Pause*) Or shame.

But he did say that it was a rewarding life, working in news. If you could keep your swelled head and your desires under control.

Kate said, He said *that*. I think that's the strangest remark I've ever heard.

*Weird.*

What kind of man was he, your father?

I've told you, I said. A good one.

Impatient, hard-working.

And loyal to a fault.

Lowell, she said. Lowell, Lowell.

The point isn't to control your *desires*.

That's the *news* you're talking about. News doesn't have anything to do with life.

It's just news.

News is what happens to someone else, she said.

And then she said, Lowell? Some time in your life you're going to have to step out of the newsroom. It's stifling in there. It's a morgue!

*Desires*, she said, and laughed again.

Honest to gosh, if I didn't know you better. If I didn't know you pretty well. I'd say you were the kind of man who makes love in the dark with his clothes on.

I'm not, I said. As you well know.

She said, Sometimes you make too much of things.

You and your clean leads.

Check it out, you say.

Then believe.

What kind of a way is that to live? she said.


LIMPETT *taps the Facit with his knuckles. He is doing a fair imitation of a young woman's voice.*

Take care, Lowell.

Take care of yourself.

I'm worried about you.


LIMPETT *turns to look at the Hopper print, and then back at the audience.*

She needn't worry.

I think it's safe to say she doesn't.


LIMPETT *recoils as the phone rings sharply.*

WELLBECK:

Old Great? Here's the deal. We're in a bind, and you've got to give way. Question of fairness, as I see it. We've got to give the younger folks a chance. I'm talking women and individuals of color and the Spanish-surnamed and our very own native Americans, bless their hearts. Brings diversity to our newsroom! Younger legs, younger hearts.

And smaller salaries, Lowell. So it's win-win, wouldn't you say?


LIMPETT *takes the sheet of paper from his jacket pocket and stands looking at it.*

WELLBECK:

(*continuing*)—so listen up, Lowell. What I'm proposing is controversial. It's a little bit out of your orbit, this thing I have in mind, that occurred to me only this morning, listening to our friends in the church. Thing is, you've been on the street too long. You know too much for your own good. So I think it's time to bring you inside, out of the cold and into the warm. How does that sound, Old Great?


LIMPETT *cocks an eyebrow at the telephone and continues to read.*

WELLBECK:

(*continuing*) You and Jack Laverty, same page. Page Two. Laverty left, Limpett right. Jack's got his repertory, all those afflicted souls who need his help. And you, Old Great. You'll be supervising the obits. We're putting the death notices on Page Two, and you're the fellow who'll choose who's noticed and who isn't. You'll be in charge! All those unsung heroes in our town. You're going to sing for them, Lowell. You're going to give them the send-off they deserve, their place in the sun. Christ, Lowell, Page Two'll be a fucking symphony, Jack with his violin, you with your big bass drum.

So come up close to the phone, Old Great.


LIMPETT *does not move one inch.*

I've got to know you want to do it. Want it so bad you can *taste* it.

So you've got to answer me right now. You've got about five seconds.

One.

Because this offer's not waiting.

It's finite. It expires at the count of five. *And there won't be another one.*

Two.

Oh, *merde* Lowell. My other phone's ringing.

I'm in my car. Call you right back.


LIMPETT *reaches into the desk drawer for a pack of cigarettes. He slits it open and lights one, exhaling a great cloud of smoke. He rolls up his shirtsleeves. His posture is almost that of a soldier. He glances at the sheet of paper in his jacket pocket and begins to speak.*

He doesn't understand something.

For an artisan, your work is your soul. Not just my work, any work. You cannot turn your back on your *work*. You cannot dishonor it. You cannot betray what you have believed in

43

your whole life. Even when you know the world has moved on. (*Pointing*). Would Edward Hopper denounce *Street Scene* because Warhol discovered *Marilyn Monroe*?

*The telephone rings but* LIMPETT *talks through it, but now in a distracted fashion. He turns the photograph in the silver frame so that the audience sees it.*

That's Kate and me.

Christmas party, last year.

The photograph doesn't do her justice. This photograph isn't worth a thousand words.

But no photograph ever is.

WELLBECK *has been muttering into the telephone.*

Where were we, Old Great?

We were at Two.

Three, Four.

You've got to want it *so* badly. You've got to decide something, Old Great. You're like that cowboy, can't get off his horse.

LIMPETT:

So listen.

WELLBECK:

It's the age of the motor car but you're still in the saddle, a goddamned misfit.

LIMPETT:

It's not that you grow old.

WELLBECK:

So you've got to decide to send Old Paint to the fucking glue factory and climb behind the wheel of my white convertible.

LIMPETT:

It's not even that you lose the girl.

Everyone grows old.

Everyone loses a girl.

WELLBECK:

Five.

LIMPETT:

And when they beat you up, you understand that, too.

You understand when they want to take your picture down to make room for other, more modern pieces.

WELLBECK:

Come by anytime, pick up your paycheck. And remember: When Norman Wellbeck calls, You *pick up the telephone.* Who do you think you are?


LIMPETT *seems not to have heard this; at any event, he's not paying attention to Wellbeck. Still, he has paused as the phone goes silent.*

They're trying to update the museum, that's all. They're reaching for a new generation with different tastes, and a different way of seeing things. And they know that for the price of one Hopper they can hang—two Warhols.

It's not that.

It's that you're not sure you can *live.*

Outside the news.

LIMPETT *turns to look at the wall containing his badges. He has one final truth to tell. He pulls the sheet of paper from his pocket and begins to read from it.*

A few years ago Victor and I were covering the war.

It doesn't matter which one.

And Victor, struggling—

Does it matter what he was struggling with?

Had a breakdown. Mild.

A mild breakdown.

They were able to treat it. I think it was exhaustion, mostly.

And a month later he said, Lowell.

All the stories we tell about each other?

You don't have to tell this one.

Let's keep this one to ourselves, in the family.

You know the score, Lowell.

*Christ*, don't let me down.

Because—if anyone found out, they'd ask questions and the word would spread.

Did you hear about Victor? Victor's sick.

Victor can't handle it.

Victor lost his nerve.

Isn't it a shame about Victor?

Do you remember how *steady* he was. Like a metronome. Poor old bastard.

And because we don't keep secrets in our business, the word got out.

Probably by close of business that day. Or the next.

No more news for you, Victor. You're out of the news hole. You're over the horizon. You're adrift. You're into the unknown.

(*Pause*)

His editor brought him home, put him behind a desk, and showed him off to the new kids, like a stuffed owl on the mantel.

And then—

*You* try to live without a by-line. You have only yourself, and your past, and whatever it is you believe in. When the by-line vanishes, you vanish with it.

LIMPETT *picks up a newspaper and reads from it, in a cadence.*

Victor Blaine, 62, a reporter for the Associated Press, was found dead yesterday in his apartment in Washington, D.C. The cause of death is under investigation.

Twenty-six words.

Clean, tight, short.

Looking through the words to the facts.

The space between the known and the unknown.

CURTAIN

# Wasps

## The Sting as the Kiss

WHEN she was nine, Melanie was stung by a wasp and in thirty minutes had lapsed into a coma. Her terrified mother drove her to the family doctor, who swiftly administered a heavy dose of adrenaline. Lucky girl; another thirty minutes and she might've died. An unfortunate allergy, the doctor said; for the rest of her life, Melanie would have to be alert and cautious, though she should not in any way think of herself as an invalid. The allergy was severe but not uncommon.

She'd been stung twice afterward; once when she was twelve, and once again when she was fifteen. A dose of adrenaline, self-administered, saved her both times—or she assumed it did. That was the catch. Many people outgrew this particular allergy, if "allergy" was the proper word for so menacing a condition. But the only way to discover whether she'd outgrown it was to withhold the antidote. And if she withheld the antidote it was possible she'd die. She supposed there were sophisticated medical tests that could determine her vulnerability once and for all; but she preferred to live with uncertainty. Until she was nineteen and in college she carried a small vial of adrenaline and a hypodermic needle, in the way a diabetic carries insulin. First stung at nine, then at twelve, finally at fifteen, she found significance in the three-year intervals and on her nineteenth birthday she took the vial and the hypodermic needle out of her purse and put them away. She was certain that the three-year cycle was broken, and just as certain that some other cycle or cycles would take its place.

She came to believe that in some specific way the wasp's sting and the coma that followed had transformed her nature, from free spirit to fatalist.


She believed that her life was limited at the outset, though this belief did not make her cynical or morbid. She'd merely discovered early what most people discovered late. That wasp's sting; perhaps in a perverse way it resembled the kiss of the prince that awakened Sleeping Beauty. She told her husband that she'd been given free of charge the sort of knowledge that others had to earn. That was simply that all things were not possible; if being an idealist meant having the belief that life could as easily be one way as another, then she was not an idealist. Her husband agreed with her partially, though he did not believe that the wasp's sting resembled a kiss any more than she resembled Sleeping Beauty; actually, he did not believe in metaphors of any kind.

Eric was a successful politician. They'd married when they were both twenty-five; she was working on her master's degree at the state university and Eric was the local state's attorney, youngest in the history of the district. At thirty he ran for the state House of Representatives and won and two years later for the state Senate and won, and finally, at thirty-six, challenged the elderly incumbent congressman and won that, too. Eric set no limits on himself. He seemed to carry with him natural good luck, which translated into a deft political instinct. His career was solid and marked with legislative accomplishment; a comer, his enthusiasm was infectious. His ambition was to run for the U.S. Senate and then, if he could position himself correctly, to try for a presidential nomination. The chances were remote, he conceded; but in Washington, anything was possible.

In the beginning, Eric tried to keep Melanie apart from his political life—not that she was clamoring to be part of it; she had her own concerns and did not care for notoriety. He told her, "If I'd wanted a politico for a wife I would've married Eleanor Roosevelt." But through his successive campaigns he learned that his wife was the shrewdest political adviser he had. She had a touch for it, as talented gardeners are said to have a green thumb. It was odd, the reverse of the typically successful "political" marriage. She was no help at all on the issues, and seemed indifferent to them. "Issues" had very little to do with the Washington she knew. She dealt strictly with tactics, matters of finance and alliance and patronage; she never took anything for granted, and believed in worst-case analysis. Melanie balanced accounts like an expert auditor, credit here, debit there; and she never lost sight of the future. Strangely, given her self-proclaimed fatalism, she had some faith in luck. This was because she did not believe in coincidence. Eric had been lucky often enough that it could not be coincidence anyway.

Melanie believed in hard work and keeping your word, rewarding your friends and ignoring your enemies. She thought that her husband was a good man and a very good politician, being both extroverted and audacious. Of course she was neither.

They had no children. Early in their marriage they considered adoption but for one reason or another kept putting it off. Then they discovered that they liked their life the way it was, unencumbered. They were comfortable together as a couple and Melanie was not encouraged when she saw the children of other political marriages.

Friends believed that in many ways Eric and Melanie led an ideal life, though some of them wondered what they saw in each other. It should not have been a mystery: What they "saw" was security. It is not unusual for an intensely public man to marry an intensely private woman. Or vice versa. They understood and enjoyed each other and did not cheat, one to the other. She was very much a part of his professional world, and he was sympathetic to, though puzzled by, her need for anonymity. She had no desire either for the limelight or the more subtle pleasures of gray eminence. When people laughingly (and occasionally not so laughingly) referred to her as "the brains," he smilingly agreed: Her tactical intuition was flawless. As for Melanie, she was glad to be of use and took no more notice of it than that. She believed that her practical value to him was precisely that of an expert reader of maps— no traveler herself, she nonetheless had an instinct for the political landscape. A minor talent. The main lines of her life centered around a restless search for knowledge: her reading, which she could share or not as the occasion required. The one absolute rule she had was that her privacy would in no way be violated. Washington was dangerous in that way; it was very easy to lose one's center of gravity.

One night Eric came home in an especially good temper, actually laughing out loud as he kissed her then moved to the sideboard to make drinks. She was easily seduced by his enthusiasm; Eric was fun to be around. "You won't believe it," he said. "What happened today."

She leaned against him, anxious to share his good humor. It was fortunate that although he took Washington very seriously he did not take himself seriously at all. She waited for the unbelievable.

"Witsell was in." This was a well-known television commentator who had become a friend. "We talked for an hour. He made me a proposition, which I said I would bring home to you, as the brains of this outfit." He handed her a drink and they walked into the garden. The night was warm and nearby they could hear the sounds of a cocktail party reaching its climax. They walked arm-in-arm around the garden.

She said, "Tell."

"He's sold a television idea to the network. He's going to produce and narrate. It's a big deal for him."

Melanie was suddenly wary and on guard. She did not trust journalists, Witsell any more than the others. "So?"

He shook his head, grinning. "What was the name of that Englishman? The writer; the one who wrote the book about

the Victorians? Witsell mentioned his name. You know the one
I mean—"

She said, "Lytton Strachey."

He nodded. "That's the one. Well, that's Witsell's idea.
'Eminent Washingtonians.' That's the name of the series, a
series of six half-hour specials, prime time. Beginning next fall,
if he can put them together by then. The idea is that it'll be a
portrait of the town through its, uh, inhabitants. Locating
them in the fabric of the town, you know what I mean?"

She recognized Witsell's phrases, and she knew what was
coming next. "Who are these inhabitants?"

He named a newspaper publisher, a lawyer, a diplomat, a
hostess, and an army general, and then looked at her and
laughed. "And us."

"Us?"

"Us," he said. "And it fits. Witsell's trying to square the circle.
Army, society, diplomacy, law, communications—and politics.
He wants people who'll be good subjects on film, otherwise the
series won't go. They've got to get people who'll *give* a little—"
He looked at her, but her face was turned away.

"Do you mean you, or do you mean us?"

"Us, the two of us. It makes good sense. Hell, it'll just take a
weekend. They'd follow me around at work, and you around
the house." He looked at her, waiting for a smile; but she did
not change expression. "Your part will make stunning television. Fifteen minutes of Melanie reading. Melanie turning
pages and thinking. What are you reading now? Is it still Dick-
ens? Or have you moved on to the Arabs? They sent over some
more books, by the way."

"The Spanish Civil War," she said absently.

"Well, I don't see how it can do us any harm."

Two gardens down, the cocktail party was still going strong. She leaned against the fence, looking down at her feet. "I don't think I want people looking over my shoulder all weekend. That isn't my idea of a relaxing weekend."

He said, "It would be damn good back home."

"I'm not so sure about that either."

He was surprised. "Why not, it's network. Prime time."

"How much control will you have?"

"As much control as I need. The best control of all. I know what I'll say, and what you'll say, and what I'll let them film. A Day in the Life of a Congressman. I'm going to be the one to pick the day. Some day when there'll be an issue on the floor. A good issue. An issue that we'll win, but not without a fight. Courageous Congressman on the ramparts. A good issue that'll be close—"

"Eric," she said. "Eric, Eric." She was amazed sometimes at his naiveté. In television, the subject had no control. Only the producer had control; it was a principle he could never understand. In a film of this kind everything would depend on the cut. On Witsell, and what Witsell wanted to prove.

He picked her up immediately and became doubtful. "Do you really think?"

"Yes, I do think. It's a mistake."

Something in her tone puzzled him. "For us, or for you?"

"For you," she lied.

"Melanie, I want to do it. I mean, I want us to do it. If I go in three years, *if* I go, this is good pudding back home. It's the best there is. Listen to the others." He named the other subjects again, by name and title, ticking them off on his fingers.

"These are well-known people, damn well known. Better known than me."

"I don't like it," she said.

"Why?"

"Too many chances for a slip—"

He moved away and stood looking at her, peering over the tops of his eyeglasses. "Come on, Melanie."

She said, "It's true." He made a gesture with his hands, friendly enough, but disbelieving. She sighed, helpless against his enthusiasm. "It's an invasion of privacy. It's like that squalid thing they showed over public television. That family, those pathetic—"

"No," he said. "It isn't anything like that at all. Nothing like that. The cameras are in here for one weekend."

"A camera in the bedroom, I suppose."

He laughed. "This is not an X-rated movie."

She said, "It's risky. I don't like it."

He was silent a moment. Then, "You're saying something else, Mel. I think what you're saying is that *you* don't want to do it." He reached for her hand. "Hell, Melanie—"

"Yes, that's right. I'm sorry I said the other thing."

"Okay, we're on the track now."

"I *am* sorry. I think it would be fine for you. And I think it would be all right in the district. Actually, it'll be very good in the district and the state...." Thinking it through, she decided that Witsell would have no reason to do a knife job. It wouldn't be that kind of program. She knew the way they thought. This would be an upbeat program; otherwise they would not broadcast it in prime time.

"All right, seriously. What bothers you about it?"

"It's voyeurism. I don't want some television reporter, even if I know him and he seems all right, poking around my life. Our life. Poking around the house, asking a lot of personal questions. Because they would have to do that. Poking into our life together; my connection with your career. I don't like to be pried at. It seems unnecessary. And it wasn't part of the arrangement. Why must we do this? It isn't just us, either. I don't understand why anyone does it. Let strangers rummage around—"

"You're taking it too seriously."

"But why—"

"Why not," he said, "If you're not ashamed of your life."

During the day, Melanie read. Tuesdays and Thursdays there was tennis at St. Albans, weather permitting, and Wednesday afternoons volunteer work at the Kennedy Center. She and Eric went out four or five nights a week, and often entertained friends at home, although she had a rule about that. No constituents in the house, unless the constituents were also friends. As it worked out, she and Eric were alone only about one night a week.

She read voraciously by subjects. Lately she'd become interested in the Spanish Civil War. She'd telephoned a friend at the Library of Congress, who sent a packet of books to her husband's office. Brenan, Borkenau, Thomas, Orwell, Ortega y Gasset. She was fascinated by the books and their descriptions of the Spanish people at war. The bulk of Spain, at the nether end of the European land mass; an exposed peninsula. Looked at in that way, Spain was exposed and vulnerable in a way that other European nations were not; the way Washington was not. She thought of Washington as a nation-state of the interior, protected by the Potomac River on one side and the Blue Ridge mountains on the other. The Chesapeake Bay to the east, and the vast expanse of America to the west. Washington was therefore closed and secure. Reading the histories, she was horrified at the extent to which the great powers manipulated Spain: They'd used the Spanish people as guinea pigs and the country as a laboratory for experiments in modern war. Those were conditions she'd vaguely been aware of, but now she knew the details; she had the facts, the difference between the P.O.U.M. and the P.S.U.C. and the various temperamental characteristics that divided the Catalans and the Castillians. The Russians were as bad as the Germans; the Italians were malignant; the British were merely weak. And the Americans did nothing.

She'd never thought of herself as a woman of causes. She believed her fascination with the Spanish people and the civil war was entirely disinterested and therefore sincere; there was nothing she could "gain" from it. It was a difficult point for Melanie to make, and therefore a subject that she took care to stay away from. This was one of the things that bothered her about the television program. She had spoken to Witsell about the Spanish war: Seated next to him at dinner one night, she'd foolishly mentioned this new enthusiasm. He was certain to ask her about it. And she would have to explain what it was that interested her about the Spanish war: Five or ten million people would be listening in on the conversation, eavesdropping....

She was *not* ashamed of her life; in fact she was proud of who she was and what she did. What do you do? I read. It wasn't something you could explain to a television reporter with cameras staring you in the face. How could you explain the pleasure and understanding that you received from *Bleak House*? Or the various readings, Thesiger and the others, into Arab culture and geography. There was no way that could be explained without you looking like a fool or a dilettante. The congressman's wife, reading. The point was that she had a good many identities, of which Congressman's Wife was only one. And when they asked—Describe the turning point in your life, the decisive step? What Was the Most Important Thing That Ever Happened to You, Melanie? Witsell would be intimate; everything would be on a first-name basis. She knew the way it would work. She'd say,

—I was stung by a wasp.

—Really? When was that?

—When I was nine. I almost died.

—And how did that change your life?

—I learned about fate.

—*Fascinating*. And what did you learn about fate?

—All things are not possible.

—Well, folks, isn't that interesting!

No, it was ludicrous. Too ludicrous, in fact. None of those questions would be asked. Witsell would ask her about Eric. The campaigns; his ambition. So instead of being ludicrous it would be in error. She thought that between the two, error was better. At least that way she would preserve that part of herself worth preserving.

She immersed herself in the books about Spain. Something inside her was touched. She wondered if Spain would ever be vulnerable again. Or perhaps the experience was so cata-strophic that the country and its people were immunized. They had managed to avoid World War II and every war there-after. Perhaps the results justified the act. Perhaps; who knew? She tried to put the books aside and concentrate on the admin-istrations of Franklin Roosevelt, but she could not forget them; they drew her back, the Brenan, the Borkenau, the Thomas, the Orwell, the Ortega y Gasset.

Eric asked her from time to time: All that knowledge, what do you do with it? That was the question that he asked her about the Spanish war, a month after their talk in the garden.

She'd smiled, it was not hard to explain to him. "Well, I have it. Now I know about the Spanish war. I didn't before. I don't have to do anything with it. It's mine, I have it, and no one can take it away from me. It's like asking what you do with a sun-tan. You don't do anything with it, but it's nice having it." She did not want to go beyond that, though the truth was she did not think her knowledge had any similarity to a suntan. "Do you know how many people were killed in the Spanish war?"

"I know that forty-eight thousand Americans were killed in Vietnam. Killed in action."

"Thousands," she said. "Hundreds of thousands. Maybe as many as one million dead, many of them in mass executions. There were thousands of bodies that were not even recovered. Here one day, gone the next. No trace, not even a decent bur-ial. Thousands simply disappeared."

"But what does that—"

"I like to have knowledge."

"I think you ought to be a teacher—"

"I am not a teacher," she said with a firmness that surprised her.

"I guess I'm just practical minded; you're so damn good...."
He was about to say "in the real world," but did not.

She knew what he meant. "I don't undervalue myself, Eric. I
know my opinions are sound. I have a knack for details. You tell
me the problem and I can play it out, complete with stage
directions. It's a knack, a minor talent. It's very useful to you
but it doesn't mean anything to me. I mean me personally. I'm
very glad that it's useful to you. In that way it means something to me, but not otherwise."

He said, "I thought it was more than that."

She smiled. "It isn't, really."

He looked at her bleakly. "Explain about the war."

"I can't get it out of my mind. It was so ... raw. The experience of civil war seems to have left them with a hatred of all
war. Or probably it isn't hatred. It's fear. Paralyzing fear of
another conflict. The Pyrenees separate them from the rest of
Europe. The spirit of the country seems to've remained intact.
Not so many cross-currents, though of course nothing's iso-
lated any more. Not any one thing. Everything is connected to
everything else." She laughed sourly. "There's a new generation now. Probably they have no understanding of the civil
war. Did you know that they killed 1,255 monks and priests in
the province of Barcelona alone?"

"My God, Melanie."

"There were 512 people murdered in the town of Ronda
alone in the first month of the war. And Ronda is supposed to
be the most picturesque village in the entire county."

"Well." He was confused now.

She said, "They've never had another war."

"A tragedy—"

"They've insulated themselves."

"Melanie?"

"It was both tragedy and misadventure."

He'd been waiting all evening to tell her, trying to find a moment that would disguise his own disappointment. "Melanie, you're off the hook."

"What hook?"

"It looks like Witsell's project is off. The network won't give him the backing after all. Damn shame; he'd written three scripts already. The network says it can't get the sponsors."

She looked at him. "I had a feeling it wouldn't go."

"I guess."

"It was risky."

He smiled at her. "No, you didn't. You were scared to death."

"No," she said. "Not scared to death. A little scared. Not scared to death."


They lived in a small house on Cleveland Avenue, a five-minute walk from the National Cathedral. Eric rose first, made his own breakfast, and was gone before nine in the morning. Melanie rose at eight-thirty, bathed, went downstairs for the coffee pot, then usually returned to bed to read until ten. At ten she returned to the kitchen for breakfast, bringing her book with her. The breakfast table was littered with the various sections of the *Washington Post,* the *New York Times,* the *Baltimore Sun,* and the *Wall Street Journal.* She glanced at the headlines, carefully folded the papers, and put them in the large wicker wastebasket. Then she sat down with her book and two boiled eggs.

She was reading then about the siege of the Alcazar in Toledo. The commander of the Nationalist troops inside the Alcazar was Colonel Moscardo. The leader of the rebel militia in Toledo telephoned him to say that if he did not surrender, his son would be executed. They'd captured the boy that morning. The rebel leader, Candido Cabello, told Moscardo, "So that you can see that it's true, he will speak to you." Father and son had a last conversation. "What is happening, my boy?" asked the colonel. "Nothing," answered the son. "They say they will shoot me if the Alcazar does not surrender." "If it be true," replied the colonel, "commend your soul to God, shout *Viva Espana!*, and die like a hero. Good-bye, my son. A last kiss." "Goodbye, father," answered the boy, "a very big kiss." Then Moscardo told Candido Cabello that the Alcazar would never surrender.

Melanie bent her head into her hands and wept. Could all that be explained by tragedy and misadventure?

Presently she dried her eyes and stood staring glumly into the garden. The garden was Eric's single hobby; it was blooming now with forsythia and two dogwoods and a blanket of roses over the wooden fence. She seldom walked in the garden because of her fear of wasps, though in fact she had never seen a wasp in the garden. Certainly they were there, but she had never seen one. She stood leaning against the window, staring into the colors—white, yellow, pink, amber; amber the color of gold.

… She'd been playing in the back yard the first time. She and her brother had a jungle gym in the back yard. They were playing king of the mountain, and she'd been knocked down on her back. She still remembered the abandon with which she'd played; she was a fearless girl, the tomboy of the neighbor-hood. She remembered laughing and shaking her fist, looking up at her older brother on his awkward perch. She was daring him to jump. Then the pain on her wrist, and the writhing insect. It looked big as a bird and made a terrible noise. She shook her hand violently and it flew away sluggishly, and she ran inside. She remembered that she hadn't cried. Her mother gave her a cookie and comforted her with words and put a cold compress doused with lemon on her wrist. There, it will be all right in a minute. You'll see the swelling, Melanie; your wrist will look like an egg. But there was no swelling and after fifteen minutes she'd thrown up violently. Her mother believed it was a reaction to the shock of the wasp's sting, though Melanie did not shock easily. Then she'd felt sleepy and her head began to ache. Her body commenced to tremble and abruptly she felt ice-cold. Her skin was clammy to the touch. Her thoughts were tangled and she found it difficult to speak; her body felt so cold, her tongue became thick and sticky. The last thing she remembered was her mother smiling at her, her head cocked at the familiar angle. Her mother's heart-shaped face, smiling with only a suggestion of worry. Why Melanie, it's only a wasp's sting. Does it hurt, honey? Why, Melanie! Then her sharp scream as Melanie tumbled off the chair to the linoleum floor ...

She opened the door and walked into the garden. She stood on the deck and looked at the flowers; the dogwood and the other flowers, and the slim elm to the rear. Up close to the bushes now, she inspected each blossom for wasps. The grass was cool on her bare feet. The day was so brilliant; the sun streamed into the garden. She looked at the shed next to the fence, the interior dark with split firewood. She walked toward it, thinking they'd need more wood for the winter.

She still carried the book, her thumb tucked into page 203. It was the second time she'd read it; it seemed to have a cumulative effect on her. She gazed over the tops of the houses and imagined Toledo at dusk, El Greco's Toledo dark and fabulous in the last rays of the sun. "A very big kiss." She imagined Washington in siege, a militia rampaging through the streets. She and Eric safe in the National Cathedral. No hostages of any kind. The Cathedral, unlike the Alcazar, would not fall. The assault would come at nightfall, and would not succeed.

She shook her head, that kiss; she thought all of it was connected, but could not understand how. Melanie moved closer to the woodshed, peeking in through the door to the cool interior, all in shadows. She stood staring into the dark, an odd small smile on her face. Then she backed away, aware suddenly that woodsheds contained wasps. She retreated quickly to the deck, and inside through the screen door. She stood in the kitchen looking over the garden and the low housetops beyond the fence, staring motionless like the captain of a vessel at sea. Expert auditor, what was the price of security? She glanced into the garden, smiling grimly. It was quite reasonable, given her circumstances; with all the wasps in Washington, she was quite safe.

# Born in His Time

HOW DIFFERENT this is from what his life was. Time is discontinuous, the surroundings all wrong. These are guilty ceremonies. The rear of the room, where I am seated, is in shadows. I turn to look at Carney, but his face is a mask. I am thinking of Born, my associate, my friend. I am trying to place Born in his time.

We became acquainted in the spring of 1959. He was representative of many ambitious, very bright, and physically nondescript young men then in Washington. He had graduated from Stanford University law school four years before, and was working on Capitol Hill for a Midwestern congressman. I believe that his family was well connected in Chicago, but I am not sure; Born was reluctant to discuss personal matters.

He came to us by chance. Our law firm, normally as stable

as the Republic, was in some turmoil because the senior partner had resigned to accept a Cabinet post. We'd always been
small and select, just the three principals and four junior partners. When the senior man left, two of our best clients left
with him; it developed that their loyalty was to him, not to the
firm. The departure of these clients left us with the decision of
shrinking the business or expanding it. This was a significant
decision, which was settled in a fortnight of intensive conversation; the junior men convinced us that we should enter the
marketplace, arguing that without the senior partner we'd continue to lose business. An ominous signal. Carney and I knew
that wasn't true (there are advantages to having your law partner in the president's Cabinet), but we were impressed by the
competitive spirit of the younger men. Carney was 55 and I
was 60 and we knew that in ten years' time the firm would be
dominated, and rightly so, by the younger element. There was
one other consideration, which was left moot. I think that both
Carney and I wanted to see the business grow on its own. I
mean by that on *our* own.

We went into the marketplace, and one of the first men I
interviewed was Born. Consulting my memorandum of the
conversation, I find we talked a good deal about the nature of a
Washington law practice. He was not entirely ignorant of this,
having spent several years on the Hill. I described to him the
specialties of the house, and some of the cases then on our
docket. He said it was his intention, eventually, to return to
government. He had no desire whatever for elective office, but
thought that in due course he would join the civilian side of
the defense establishment. In Washington, we call these men
inners-and-outers.

I asked him why defense, it seemed to me an odd choice, and he replied that he had a working knowledge of atomic physics. He was thinking ahead, to the time when there would be international agreements covering the uses of atomic energy. Law and physics did not go together now, but some day they would.

"How many years can you give us?" I asked, half facetiously because he was courting us and not the other way around. I had a file full of applications at this time.

He thought a moment, and replied that he could give us six years at minimum. "That's a commitment," he said.

I wanted to clear the air right away, so I was blunt. "We are not a boot camp for bureaucrats," I told him. "We are a law firm. One of the three or four best law firms in this city. The business is going to expand and we can't afford to have lawyers whose minds are distracted ... on other matters. We require 24-hour-a-day lawyers. Our clients demand it and we require it."

"Don't worry about that," he said. "I want to make plenty of money. I've got to have the money if I'm going to go into government at the level I want. I have to have money, and I've got to know the right people. You'll get 24 hours and more from me. I'll tell you honestly, I love the law. If you'll give me a try, Mr. Weiss, I'll make good."

I liked his candor and what seemed to me an admirable confidence. He was a young man who knew what he wanted. "What are your salary requirements?"

"Twenty," he said without hesitation.

"You have a wife?" Twenty thousand dollars was on the high side.

"Yes, no children."

I nodded and asked him the details of his Hill experience. I already knew it, but I wanted his version. He'd come highly recommended but I wanted to make certain he wasn't another fat cat's nephew. It developed that Born was the congressman's principal legislative assistant, and had dealt mainly with two important committees: Appropriations and Commerce. He knew the people, he said, and the manner in which the committees operated. He knew the details, and in two years' time had come to know the most powerful members and their interests, public and private.

"I know the Hill cold," he said.

I should explain that our firm was characteristic of a certain kind of Washington law practice. We very seldom appeared as attorneys of record; that is to say, we rarely represented clients before the various commissions or the federal courts. We advised our clients on approaches to the law: A man wanted to get from here to there, and we told him how to do it. When it actually came to appearing before the Federal Communications Commission or the National Labor Relations Board or the Justice Department or the Congress, we would pass that on to one of the larger firms, which had the staff and the research facilities for what, inevitably, would be extended proceedings. Some of this work was *ex parte*, and my partner, Carney, handled it in his own way and I did not interfere. Carney was an extremely able lawyer, but briefs and research bored him. He was not so much a lawyer as a man who *practiced law*, and there's a considerable difference between the two.

To his credit, Carney could sometimes accomplish more in

an afternoon at Burning Tree than I could in a week of research. I was a lawyer's lawyer, specializing in antitrust; pleasure to me was an afternoon spent searching for precedent. To Carney it was a round of golf or a game of bridge with the director of the Internal Revenue Service or a ranking member of the House Agriculture Committee. A law firm in Washington needs both kinds of men, and the division of labor between us worked out splendidly. At any event, at this point in my conversation with Born, I left my office to consult with Carney.

"The young fellow from Fletcher's staff is in my office," I told him. "Do you want to take a look?"

"What do you think?"

"A quality man."

"How long on the Hill?"

"Two years. He talks as if he knows everyone there."

"He might at that," Carney said. "I've already spoken to Fletcher. Quite by accident I saw him at lunch. Fletcher says he's the genuine article, sorry to lose him. Smart, extremely hard worker. A bit innocent, Fletcher says, but willing to learn. It seems to me that it would be useful to have a man close, familiar ... with that side of the Hill. Don't you think?"

"Assuredly," I said.

"If we get the golden apple"—this, a reference to a potential client, a large private foundation due to come under government scrutiny—"we'll need more help on that side of the Hill." Carney smiled. "I think he sounds fine."

"I agree," I said.

"But I better talk to him anyway. Get the feel."

"He wants twenty to start."

"Does he now?"

"That's what he says."

"Commendable ambition," Carney said. "I think eighteen-five will do."

We hired Born that afternoon.


I look back on what I have written and it occurs to me that there may be a misunderstanding. I refer to Carney's role in our firm. Through the animadversions of the press, particularly the Washington press, the public has an entirely false impression of the Washington lawyer. "A black bag operation," as the muckrakers put it: payoffs, bribes, influence peddling and the like. I do not deny that it sometimes happens, but it does not happen in our firm. To understand Washington law, one must understand the nature of the federal bureaucracy and the urgent demands of clients. Briefly, time is money.

Consider: there are perhaps one dozen top-of-the-line law firms in this town, and Carney, Weiss is one of those. Clients come to us with complicated problems, and it is my job to know the law. I proceed to build a case to achieve the client's objective or to thwart the objective of the client's enemies: offensive law, defensive law. Either way, the primary difficulty is one of access. Whether it is a matter before a committee of Congress, the Internal Revenue Service, or one of the executive departments or agencies, our client goes to the bottom of a bureaucrat's in-basket. He loses time. Time is money.

Now it happens that Carney knows the bureaucracy, the men who turn the wheels. Some of them he has known since the New Deal. A telephone call can get a client from the bottom of the stack to the top (or, as sometimes happens, the reverse). Sometimes an interview can solve a client's problem. Carney is very adroit at these arrangements, which require a good deal of discretion. Of course at the point of contact the question becomes one of law, what is feasible and what is not, what is *practical* in the circumstances. At that point the client takes his chances like any other citizen. But Carney's is the decisive move, and one reason why our firm has retained the confidence of important men for so many years. Since it's only a question of bureaucracy, is there anything sinister about that? The question answers itself.

I grew fond of Born, and eventually came to look on him as something of a protégé. I took pains to review his work, and to offer suggestions from time to time. But I am heuristic in my view of the education of a lawyer, and encouraged Born not to take my word or Carney's, but to find out for himself. I have never seen a young man work harder or with greater concentration. It was difficult for him because he labored under a ponderous writing style that depended heavily on paradox and contradiction. He was rather too enamored of theory, which as an attitude can be crippling. It was simply his cast of mind, which in time took its toll. He did not have a genius for the law, by which I mean an instinct, a style of inquiry that leads a man to the knot of a problem. I am fond of Steele's unkind aphorism, which is a call to tenacity. *What's the first excellence of a lawyer? Tautology. What the second? Tautology. What the third? Tautology.* Born had no gift for the obvious.

But he worked so hard and to such generally good effect that in three years he was made a full partner. He was then 32, the youngest partner in the firm. As we expected, our business did grow and Born was now one of eight full partners. I am a widower and something of a bear for work myself, so late at night in the office we'd have a drink together, when the chores were done, and sit and talk. Our conversations centered mostly on work, and I must say it was pleasure listening to him dissect a case. He was tireless, and what fascinated him were the approaches to the law. I mean the various weapons used to attack or defend a position. He was not a genuine advocate because he was not a passionate man, at least not then. I would argue with him that the approach was only half of it, and often less than half. The important part of the practice of law was the skill and energy with which a man *pursued*. Having first prepared the battlefield.

One night quite late I fell to reminiscing about the beginnings of the firm. The third senior partner had been a close personal friend of Mr. Roosevelt. He knew everyone in Washington and established our business with a solid foundation of private clients. Family accounts, wills, trusts, that sort of thing. But no law firm ever grew rich on that, so he brought in Carney and me to handle corporate accounts. One way or another, that's political law and it was quite by chance that Carney and I meshed so well.

By 1948, I told Born, "we could pick and choose our cases, and believe me we picked and chose with quite a bit of care. A few years ago, I'd guess that half our income was from other lawyers. *Their* clients just wanting Carney, Weiss in on the case. Carney outside, me inside."

"Security blanket," Born laughed.

"Well, they believe in added insurance. And in his field, Carney's the rock of Prudential."

Born leaned across the desk then, and asked very seriously: "Tell me this. Can Carney really deliver?"

"Yes, but that isn't the point. What it is, is a track record. When Carney's in on the case, a client feels more secure. Carney comes high, but when a man has a couple of million dollars at stake, another ten or twenty thousand—or fifty or seventy thousand—doesn't bother him. He wants to win, and it doesn't matter how much it costs. Tax deductible, anyway."

"And he never appears as the attorney of record."

"Hell, no. He's 'of counsel' and sometimes not that. Sometimes he doesn't appear at all, on *any* record. I review the approach, and Carney talks to the client. Sometimes that's all there is to it."

"Sometimes he makes a telephone call."

I smiled and shrugged. That was Carney's affair.

"Personal contact," Born said.

I thought then that I ought to set the young man straight. Young men do not see events in proportion; they tend to dramatize. What was it that Dr. Johnson said? 'It is natural for young men to be vehement, acrimonious and severe.' I leaned across the desk. "First of all, they are not hiring Carney alone. They are hiring the firm. People tend to over-value the personal contacts. They're useful, but if the case is patently no good they're not worth a damn. You have to have a *case*, something plausible. Nevertheless..." I laughed, there were some amusing aspects to Carney's work. "Books do furnish a room, and witchdoctors do cast a spell. There's definitely something ... incantatory ... about what Carney does."

"A rainmaker," Born said.

"Yes, and sometimes his reputation works to his disadvantage. Some years ago an insurance company presented an extremely complicated proposal before him. I mean it was *extremely* complicated; even the company's lawyers were confused at one or two points. Carney studied the proposal and counseled them to do nothing. And submitted a very large bill. This company thought that Carney had ... deceived them, and promptly went to another firm, which set about implementing the proposal. It is quite accurate that Carney did not understand what had been put before him, but what he did understand—as the client did not—was that the problem would soon be rectified by legislation. There was a bill buried away in a committee of the Congress. That insurance company spent ten times Carney's fee in its eventually needless ... agitation. Carney's advice was as good as gold. Doing nothing is often the wisest course."

Born smiled, then looked at me directly. "Carney's law," he said. "Doesn't it seem old-fashioned? Doesn't it seem an anachronism to you?"

"No," I said. "Have you looked at the accounts book this year?" He did not press the point, but fell silent. I watched him for a moment, then asked suddenly: "Do you like the work? What you do here."

"Sometimes," he said.

"Not exactly a bell-ringing endorsement. How can you work as hard as you do at something you're lukewarm about?"

"Oh, I'm not lukewarm," he said hastily. "I do it in isolation. And as a matter of fact, I do like it. I don't think I could do what Carney does, though."

"It's a special talent," I agreed.

He lit a cigarette and I looked at him again, closely, as if seeing him for the first time. Stubble was coming up on his chin, and his eyes were deep-set and circled. His fingers were mahogany with nicotine. His pallor was almost frightening, but with all this his face remained youthful, unlined, and alert.

"What does your wife think of this, the long hours?"

"She doesn't mind," Born said.

I said nothing to that, because I had been through it before with young men in our firm. There were two answers, yes she does mind, or no she doesn't. Either way, it was a prescription for trouble.

Born read my silence, and sought to reassure me. "You don't know her; she understands. She knows the score. The law is a jealous mistress."

*That* old saw; I wasn't sure what he meant. I was on the brink of delivering my lecture on wives, but decided not to. One couldn't become embroiled in the personal lives of one's associates. It never did any good, and more often than not led to bad blood.

"It's true all right," he said.

I smiled. No argument.

"We're two very determined people. We've set our goals; we know what we want."

"Money," I laughed.

"More than money," he said.

"What else then?"

77

He stamped out the cigarette in the ashtray, and frowned. No answer. Instead, he invited me to his apartment for a drink and I accepted.

They lived in an apartment building in Georgetown, situated only a few blocks from my house. Immediately when we entered the foyer I was sorry that I'd come. The hallway was dark and cold, and there was no noise coming from any part of the building. I knew his wife would be asleep and the last person she wanted to meet was the senior partner from her husband's law firm. I knew the pattern there, too. Embarrassment and excuses. Either the apartment would be tidy in which case she would be defiant, or it would be untidy in which case she would be apologetic. I thought of my own study, lined with books, and my present reading: Volume II of the memoirs of Saint-Simon. The book was one of the full set left me by my wife; it is a leather bound set, printed on heavy vellum. I longed at that moment to be sitting in my big chair, the lamp on, a Scotch and seltzer nearby, reading Saint-Simon with care. I amused myself with these thoughts as we silently mounted the stairs. In any event, I need not have concerned myself. The apartment was quite neat. And quite empty. Mrs. Born was not at home.

On the occasion of the firm's 40th anniversary we arranged a reception at the brownstone. There was a good deal of discussion about it, because I wanted something small and manageable and Carney wanted a spectacle. When the idea was first proposed, it was to invite a few clients to come round some afternoon at five for a cocktail and a canapé. But Carney prepared a list of 500 people, ranging from the chief justice of the United States to the chief of police of the District of Columbia. As I have indicated, Carney knew everyone.

The affair was a bit spectacular for my case, but the partners seemed to want it, so I acquiesced. The firm was doing well; we had successfully managed the transition from small-caliber to large without sacrificing quality. We were now heavily involved in broadcast law, and Carney had undertaken two extremely delicate assignments on behalf of a South American head of state. I have no taste for celebrity, none at all—but I confess a certain pride in seeing the firm favorably mentioned in the pages of *Fortune*.

But to return to the reception. At five in the afternoon, they began drifting in. Clients, senior partners of other firms, newspaper editors, government bureaucrats. I counted half a dozen senators, the attorney general, and two justices of the Court (as it turned out, the chief justice was traveling and unable to be with us: but he sent a friendly telegram). We did it properly, too, with a dozen waiters and fresh hors d'oeuvres and the best liquors. It was on this occasion that I first met Born's wife.

She walked up to me and introduced herself straight away. I found myself looking into the eyes of a tall, dark-haired girl, very severely dressed, but possessed of an enchanting smile. I immediately connected the two of them; they seemed to fit somehow. I said I was very happy to meet her, and she grinned.

"My husband talks about you all the time."

"He and I," I said. "We share a passion for late-night work."

She laughed gaily, and touched my sleeve. "It's too bad about your nepotism rule. We could all work late at night, then."

I did not understand the reference, and nodded politely.

"We could all work late at night at the brownstone," she repeated. Then she saw the puzzled look on my face, and added: "I'm a lawyer, too."

"Your husband never told me that."

"Ah, didn't he?"

"Perhaps he did," I said. "Perhaps I'd forgotten."

She smiled at me again, a bit wickedly I thought. We both knew that her husband had never, in any way, hinted that his wife was an attorney. I knew that she worked, but I assumed that it was in a secretarial capacity. I must say I was surprised. I asked her whom she worked for, and she named a firm down the street. It was not one of the quality firms. She leaned very close to me then, and said softly that she was about to change jobs. I bent to hear her; the noise was growing in volume.

"I'm joining the legal section of the State Department," she said.

"Well, congratulations."

"I'll be the only woman there."

I was really quite astonished, because the legal section of the Department was difficult to enter without political sponsorship of some kind. In fact, the section was something of a plum. My demeanor must have suggested this to her.

"No, I have no political clout. But I'm a good lawyer."

"You must be, to move to the State Department. At your age."

"Age and sex," she said quickly.

"Yes," I said. "That, too."

She was so very pretty that I felt immediately drawn to her. She had a manner older than her years, despite her miniskirt and provocative language. There was something dashing about her; she was a woman with a flair.

"What will you do there? One of my closest friends was legal counsel for the Department. But he's been dead many years."

"I don't really know," she said. "It doesn't matter. They screw around with you the first year. I'm very anxious to move out, to see other worlds. I'm always excited at a new job. The firm I'm with now, it's a cats-and-dogs outfit." She was watching me carefully. Then she took a drink from a passing waiter and smiled again. "My husband admires you."

"Well, that's good of him. It was a good day for the firm ..."

"He said you were a gentleman and a scholar."

"Yes, well ..."

"He brought you to my apartment once. It was some time ago."

"Yes, I'm afraid it was quite late."

"I wasn't there."

There was something aggressive in her voice and manner, and I did not reply. I am an older widower now, almost 60 years old. My wife would know how to deal with aggressive women. My wife was quite shy, but also very sure of herself. Born's wife combined aggression and sexuality in amazing combination.

"No, you weren't."

"Well," she said brightly, "I guess I'll go look for Born."

We did not speak again until the end of the evening. It was about nine o'clock before the last of them were shuffled out the door. The rest of us, the partners and their wives, were sitting quietly in the reception room having a final drink and congratulating ourselves on the success of the party. Born and his wife were near the door, listening to the conversation. At length, as we all got up to go, they came over to say good night.

"An excellent affair," I said.

"Wonderful." Born was excited. "Did you see the justices? The AG came with his wife. We had everyone in town. My God, you could've held a Senate caucus at one point, *including* the lobbyists. I doubt if there was a law firm in this town that wasn't represented. Anyway, the better ones…"

"You never told me your wife was a lawyer."

"Didn't I?" He seemed surprised, and bent to brush some cigarette ash from the front of his vest. "Didn't I? Well, she is. And a damned good one, too."

"And now with a new job."

He turned toward her, perplexed, clearly off balance. "What new job is that?"

"I got the State Department job," she said quietly.

He said nothing at first, then dipped his head. The silence was awkward for me, and I said something light to relieve it. Born either didn't hear me, or chose not to acknowledge it. He stood for a few moments looking at her, his face a mask now.

"Which one was it?"

"Legal section," she said. "Less money than I'm making now, but a better job. *Much* better. And there'll be some travel, too, I got that assurance today, as a promise."

"Congratulations," he said, and turned to me with a shy smile. "It's the job we've been waiting for."

"*I've* been waiting for," she said.

"The application has been in for some time. A friend of ours is deputy in the legal section. You know how it works; he's been looking after the application."

"I applied last month," she said. She looked at Born, and then at me. "I got word this morning. At the office. I can report for work in three weeks."

"Good-o," he said.

I left them like that, got my hat and coat, and hurried out of the office. Lawyers often make odd marriages, but the Borns' were the oddest in my experience.


I would see them from time to time at large receptions, sometimes alone, sometimes together. In the early 1960s Washington was as fresh and exciting as any capital in Europe. The European comparison was often made, though not by Born. They'd apparently built a public life and had a wide circle of friends, most of them from the political and diplomatic worlds. Three nights a week they made the rounds of the embassies, the other nights "spent"—her word—at private houses, in candlelit dining rooms in Georgetown and Cleveland Park, quiet suppers for six or eight in backyard gardens. Talk centered around the personalities of the men inside the administration. At that time even the monuments appeared to be the personal property of those who lived in the capital, and there were glamorous comparisons: Paris, London. The sense of awe and power is nothing new to Washington, but in the early 1960s there was one other quality: *chic*. I have never seen anything quite like it, before or since. The milieu was political, *tactical* Born said; it was tactics, not strategy, that made a successful life.

He and his wife cultivated the powerful not for reasons of glamour or status but because the powerful made the town go.

Know the sources of power, know the town. Pointless to live in Washington without knowing who ran it, as pointless as living in Hollywood without knowing film producers. Or that was the way Born explained it, believing that he was saying something original and revealing. Truthfully, I believe he was uneasy. But it was a familiar argument to anyone acquainted with the capital. Henry Adams was a connoisseur of ambition in its various forms and how that, in turn, related to power. Adams knew Washington as well as anyone, and believed at the end of his life that power was poisonous.

So Born settled into his fourth-floor office at Carney, Weiss. The firm had its own style like any good club, and Born fitted in. His days were rituals that became ceremonies: a man of habit, each morning he'd hail the Q Street bus and ride to the brownstone on Massachusetts Avenue, on the way digesting the Washington morning newspaper. Inside the building, he'd collect his mail at the receptionist's desk, and ring for the tiny elevator that took him to his office. The brownstone smelled of ink and valuable carpets; its ceilings were high and in places they were peeling. Alighting at the fourth floor, Born would greet the secretaries and any partners strolling the halls. Early each morning, the senior men conferred in Carney's small corner office. I should explain that all the offices were small except those of the very junior partners, which were quite large. This was a tradition of the firm; the senior men always had the smallest offices, which as it happened were also corner offices with oak paneling and marble fireplaces. On the occasions when Born was invited to join us, he would slip quietly through the door, pour a cup of coffee, relax in an armchair, and admire Carney's etchings—not precious little Vanity Fair prints, but political cartoons, celebrations of chicanery. Nast. Herblock. Mauldin. And one reproduction: an innocent landscape, Cézanne in Provence.

The firm and its processes became Born's life. The battered secondhand desk and freshly filled cigarette box. The long yellow legal pads. The Faber No. 2 pencils. The twin Parkers poised like artillery in an onyx plinth. The creamy stationery with the names of the partners in sleek black, upper left. And his own files, his pieces of the whole. The law itself was an environment, its very language an exquisite description of balance. Statute, precedent, jurisdiction, affidavit: Latinate words, *habeas corpus, fieri facias*. Soaring, poetic in their way.

This was a world of promontories and depths, shoals, wreckage, beacons. He exulted in the truly difficult cases where four or five partners would meet to navigate the approach, all of them working together in harmony and discipline. And each heavily dependent on the others, for hasty or immature advice in one area could ruin the case for everyone. Born loved complexity.

Apart from the firm's business, he had four or five individual clients—friends for whom he'd written wills or filed minor suits or whom he had advised in one way or another. He seemed to take a special delight in solving personal problems, and the more personal the better. Once when close friends decided to divorce he undertook to represent the wife and urged the husband to hire Mrs. Born. The Borns could work it out to everyone's satisfaction, and he promised a reasonable fee. When Born's wife reminded him that such a procedure was a violation of every known legal ethic, he shrugged and said that they would be doing a service for friends—and wasn't that the important thing? Wasn't that what the law was all about?

In his mid-30s now, Born felt he was working at the top of his talent. He balanced the big clients with the small, each case acquiring its own personality and containing its own particular challenge. All these things were part of the fabric of his life, the legal method strikingly similar, the initial meeting in the office with the problem explained (and Born's first question, briskly put: "What is it that you want to do?"), notes taken on the legal pads, the appropriate law thoroughly and lucidly explained, and all of it subsequently filed in heavy manila folders. Born filed everything, turning aside complaints from the other partners ... *My God you don't have to squirrel away every scrap of paper!* Born disagreed. He saved string on all clients, assembling their biographies, taking notes of casual meetings and telephone calls, and preserving cuttings from newspapers and magazines and the law journals. His office was heaped with paper, the bookcases filled to overflowing.

After nine years at it, I believe that Born was unable to separate what he did from the atmosphere in which he did it. This was an atmosphere of trust and familiarity. In time, the junior partners naturally divided into inside men and outside men. Weiss men and Carney men. Working for Carney meant long hours of intense investigation, arduous searches for legal and political precedent—"I want a skeleton from every closet," Carney'd say, believing as he did that the government was a fabulous ossuary. The law was one thing and the men who administered it quite another; Carney law presumed a knowledge of both categories. Carney's men would supply him with memos (the voting record of a congressman, the business interests of a member of the regulatory agencies; one thing and another), and from that he would extract odd facts while pursuing his informal contacts.

As the firm grew, Born found himself occasionally on Carney's side of the fence, and learned a new dimension to the tautological art. Carney: always courteous, always aggressive, always certain of direction; always confident that laws and men were elastic. Born began to enjoy his occasional patrols into Carney's world of hard realism. The quiet visits to the Executive Office Building, telephone calls at the end of the day (Born listening in on a second line, making notes in shorthand), cocktails at the Metropolitan Club, long afternoons on the links at Burning Tree. I think Carney was always a little amused by Born—so serious, so grave of mind. But Carney trusted him, so it developed that Born had a foot in both camps, the trusted associate of us both. This was most unusual. Carney and I, we practiced different law.

I have explained that as a firm, Carney, Weiss, attempted to stay in the background. This was one of the traditions of the firm, although with size it became increasingly difficult to adhere to it. It became a tradition more honored in the breach. From time to time Carney undertook work of an overtly political nature, and this was always done privately. Carney and I had an unspoken agreement that his political work was *ex parte*, and not to be confused with the firm (although, of course, the fees were shared). This is an example of what I mean. Some time ago one of the truly disreputable hangers-on in Washington sold his memoirs to a prominent publishing house for several hundred thousand dollars. This man was a liar, and on behalf of several gentlemen then in government Carney undertook to convince the publishers that the material was libelous and the contract therefore invalid. He prevailed, and the book was never published; the hanger-on was compensated for his time (a handsome sum, I might add), and in due course the matter was forgotten. Well, that is not precisely accurate. Sine it had received no publicity, it hardly could have been "forgotten." No one knew of it, except the principals and Carney and of course me. One intriguing fact about Carney: he knew every prominent newspaperman in town, and was generous about granting interviews. But when he was working on a delicate matter, he was a tomb of secrets.

I mention this as preamble to the Maxey affair, as partial explanation why the case came to us. And why I was so concerned, since to accept it meant a complete break with our traditions. This was in the spring. I was in Carney's office, seated in the red leather client's chair. Carney was at the window, his hands in his pockets, talking into a telephone he'd jammed between his ear and his shoulder. When Born stepped through the door, Carney put a finger to his lips. Quiet.

"... yes, sir," Carney was saying at intervals with rare—I daresay unprecedented—deference. He turned to Born and lifted his eyebrows. "We understand the importance ..."

"Tell him we aren't equipped," I said. "Tell him we don't have the staff. The case is *messy*." I spoke loudly, in hopes that my words would carry over the telephone.

Carney shook his head. He spoke into the receiver again. "It'll be difficult, I want to level with you ..." The other must have cut him off, because Carney fell silent, his head nodding. Born lit a cigarette, and passed the package to me.

"I gather you're not about to take no for an answer," Carney said, and smiled. "I had that impression, yes. That's the definite impression I'm getting."

"No, for God's sake," I groaned.

"Well, Weiss will be handling all the research. The law of the matter. He's better at that than I am, better than anyone in town, in fact. I'll be out front. But it's been a long time for both of us ..."

There was no way to derail Carney, so I simply sat back and shook my head.

"... we'll do it entirely in-house, yes," Carney said. Another pause. "Weiss and I and a young man named Born, used to work for Bill Fletcher on the Hill." Carney wheeled and winked at Born. "I'll do what I can ..." He paused again, and held the telephone out in front of him. The voice scratched loudly, and was silent. "I mean *all* I can, yes. The hearing's tomorrow, and from what I understand it will be most difficult. Maximum difficulty. I do want it completely understood that we are not prepared for this, and can offer no guarantees ..."

Another pause, longer this time. Carney listened carefully and nodded, and then lowered his voice. "Well, that's very generous of you. I must ask that we have everything in this office by noon today. All the files, and Mr. Maxey. Most particularly Mr. Maxey. We're not at all prepared for this. We've not followed it in any detailed way; all we know is what we've read in the newspapers. Can we—I mean, can *you*—get them to hold over the hearings until next week?"

"Let me talk to him one minute," I said, and reached for the telephone.

"Yes," Carney said, turning toward the window.

"One minute—."

"We'll do our best," Carney said hastily, and hung up. Then he turned to me. He was smiling broadly, standing at attention behind his desk. "He hung up on me," Carney said. "I couldn't hold him."

"You didn't put up much argument."

"He thinks he can get the hearings laid over."

"You didn't put up any argument at all."

"I told him we couldn't guarantee anything. He has that message loud and clear. There was no option. How the hell do you say no? He put it in such a way that a refusal was not possible. Look at it this way. We're serving the national interest. We're paying our dues." Carney smiled. "And *he* will pay *his* Q.E.D."

Born was just a third party in the room now. This was between Carney and me. "It's a lost cause," I said. "No matter how much business this brings in, nor how many IOUs you collect. Maxey's a lost cause. This case has mud on it." Something prevented me from adding the obvious: Carney had brought us over an invisible line. We were now out front on a political matter.

"We may win it," Carney said.

"No, we won't," I said. "There's no chance of that."

He was thinking now, staring out the window. Absently, he replied: "Well, I committed us."

"You certainly did."

"Look, you understand something. That man's a bad enemy. He's the worst enemy you can have."

I said nothing to that, because it was true.

In the silence that followed, Born spoke for the first time. He was flushed and excited; he'd never seen Carney and me in serious argument. I suppose it was similar to the first time a child sees his parents in serious disagreement. Born turned to Carney and asked him what we were talking about.

"Willard Maxey," I said, and looked at Carney.

Carney smiled, and nodded at the telephone. "That was the president."

Born said, "Well, well."

## II

The hearings consumed six weeks and 20 witnesses, and after the first week Weiss began to back away. The Maxey affair was not a question of law, but a question of politics; Weiss detested its nuances. Carney and Born took over the case. Born's days began at 6 and ended at 1 or 2 in the morning. Often he slept in his office, on a soft leather couch positioned between two filing cabinets. His other work went off his calendar, and was distributed among the junior partners. He talked with his wife every day or two, usually late at night from the office. He was guarded in his own conversation, but she reported to him the details of her job at the State Department. He listened distractedly, nodding his head and saying the appropriate things. Good. That's wonderful. Dandy. For himself, he felt the hearings becoming an obsession.

"How's it going?" she'd ask. "I saw you on television today; you looked tired. Your suit wasn't pressed. You shouldn't hunch so. You hunch so over the table, it makes you look old ..."

"I can't talk."

"The phone bugged?"

"I assume so."

"Talk in code," she'd say. "Use the old code."

Born laughed wearily.

"Can't you remember it?"

"We're all paying our dues," he said.

"I don't get the reference."

"It's a new code."

At the end, the proceedings became a minuet, a dance to the music of time. Neither the opposition nor the president's friends were prepared to move in close and cut it off. The days seemed interminable. Carney and Born came to the caucus room of the Old Senate Office Building each morning, chatted amiably with the press, and waited for the committee chairman to call the hearing to order. The room was stuffed with television people and their paraphernalia, as if what were at stake was a nomination to the Supreme Court or the Cabinet; but it was neither of those, it was a simple federal judgeship. In the last weeks there were frequent interruptions—a holiday recess, illnesses, excuses of various kinds. It seemed impossible to let go. The outcome was never in doubt after Senator Fletcher's dramatic statement, his personal leave-taking, which came in an exclusive interview with a television personality. *After reviewing all the facts, I can no longer stand behind Willard Maxey.*

"When you hear them talk about 'reviewing all the facts,'" Carney muttered sourly, "then you can retire to a neutral corner."

The committee refused to close down the hearings, on the

theory that every minute of television time cost the president votes. So it remained for Carney, Born, and Weiss to convince the nominee to voluntarily withdraw his name. Carney was working to extricate the president, to get him off his own hook. But Maxey refused to cooperate; he remained opaque and immovable.

He sported heavy shades from the beginning and when Carney and Weiss talked seriously to him it was like peering into a reflecting pool: two black mirrors in a round black face made maddening by a set smile behind a hedge of bone-white teeth. Carney and Weiss attempted every persuasion they knew, only to be refused by Maxey in his put-on watermelon accent (he'd learned law and how to circumvent it at New York University Law School in the nineteen-thirties; his acquaintance with the South was limited to the hotels of Miami Beach).

"No way," Maxey'd say. "No, man. I can't *do* it. I have my people to think of, all those good mothers who've gone down the line in defense of one of their own. Who want to see a dude on the federal *bench*."

"But Judge Maxey," Weiss replied, preserving the formalities to the end, not getting the point, unable to comprehend what his client implied. "Judge Maxey, it's the president who wants you to resign. It's an embarrassment to him now. We're losing this case. You must see that yourself. We've done our best, but we can't pull it off. We have no support. We can't win!"

Maxey shook his head, shocked and saddened. "I can't believe that, Mr. Weiss. I *do not* countenance it. Why, this is a solemn proceeding before a committee of the Congress! And if the president wants what you say he wants, if he wants me out — why won't he tell me (pause, wide smile, glistening teeth) *hisseff?* My calls, gentlemen—gentlemen, my calls are refused at the White House! I can't get him on the telephone!"

"A busy man," Weiss said sympathetically.

"Absolutely," Born agreed.

Carney said patiently, "We haven't got the troops."

Willard Maxey glared at Carney, then spoke coldly: "Mr. Carney. The troops may have left the battlefield. But they are not going to shoot the wounded."

Then Carney, who thought he knew exactly what was happening, turned to his partner and spoke quietly. "Let Willard and I and Born here talk privately for a moment. I think we can reason together on this matter. In fact, I'm confident of it. Let me call you when we've reached a meeting of minds."

"My conscience," Maxey began.

Weiss heard Carney speak soothingly, as he left the room, closing the door softly behind him. "Conscience," he heard Carney say. "A good thing, a valuable thing, an expensive trait of character. How much do you suppose it's worth?"


Born had lived up to all expectations, and more. He was tireless, a lawyer on an exhaustive search for fact and precedent. No approach was left unexamined. He reviewed the history of Senate investigating committees, to little profit. He assembled depositions from friends and enemies. When Carney needed a fact for his weekend golf game, it was Born who supplied it; when Carney needed precedents for his line of attack at the hearing, it was Born who researched the brief. He made the case for Maxey in a bluntly worded memorandum quietly distributed to half a dozen influential newspapermen. Through all this drifted the man himself, fifth business at the entertainment. Maxey watched Born with muscular amusement, occasionally correcting a detail, but rarely volunteering information. He gave the impression of a large and dangerous beast, docile for the moment but restless. Maxey's latent energy was palpable.

Exhausted at the end of it, knowing they had lost, Born went to Bill Fletcher on his own to convince him to reverse himself, and stay the course. He had worked so single-mindedly on the case that he was now convinced of his client's essential innocence, though willing to believe he was unqualified for the federal bench—if the standard was Holmes or Learned Hand. But that was not the point, as he told Fletcher. A subtle appreciation of Constitutional Law was not the issue. Ability was. Experience. Probity ...

"Probity, my ass," Fletcher said.

"Bill, when I was working for you in the House ..."

"Different game, friend. This is the Senate now. You screw around with some things, not with this."

"Bill, for God's sakes! This is the president's friend and ally. If you desert him now, it'll be the end. I understand your problems. You may not like Willard Maxey. I don't, much. But no one has proved him a criminal, beyond reasonable doubt...."

"President made a mistake," Fletcher said. "We all do. He should force Maxey out. Right now."

Born reiterated the familiar arguments, but Fletcher shook his head, adamant. "Why are you giving me all this heat? I know how you and Carney came to represent Maxey. You've done your job, done it well. No one holds you responsible. Don't *lean* so hard. I get your point. I heard you out, and I don't agree. Go back and tell Carney I'm a son-of-a-bitch. Let's have a drink and be friends and forget about it."

But Born could not relent; he'd come to admire Willard Maxey. In the witness chair, Maxey was a model of chilly self-confidence, a sullen sacristan guarding the vessels of his reputation. Not once did he turn to his attorneys for their advice and counsel. He never explained nor excused nor defended the details of his life. When the chairman of the committee embarked on a rambling question related to an indictment 30 years before, Maxey listened coldly and with apparent indifference. And made no reply.

—Will the witness respond?

—To what?

—The charges, sir!

—You have read them.

—And what is your answer?

—As you said, they are charges.

— ... one second, please, sir!

—You can charge anything you like.

—There were several charges, a number of them ...

—*Summum jus, summa injuria.*

The chairman leaned forward, a hand cupped to his ear.

—What was that?

—An old *Harlem* adage, Senator. A favorite along the curbstones. Known and known well to black *mothers*. Dudes ...

Maxey leaned into the microphone then, and looked closely at each member of the committee. He whispered the words, in a tone so menacing that the hearing room immediately fell still. Pure theater, as Carney said later—the battle won, the war lost. "The more law, the less justice," Maxey translated, and his supporters—accustomed to a rougher version—met the words in silence, let them hang for a moment, then whooped and cheered from the benches in the rear of the room.

Born, believing that he understood the value of Willard Maxey, worked on Fletcher. Midway through the hearings they talked for an hour one afternoon in the lounge of the Metropolitan Club. Born granted the objections, the cloud of the indictments, the suspicions—or virtual certainties—that his client was involved in the rackets. Granted! Adopting Maxey vernacular, Born told Fletcher that there was no question, none at all, that the judge (he sat then on a lower court in Manhattan) was a bad-ass, a hardcase—"one tough nigger," Born said, no paradigm, and that was just the point. Maxey'd lived in the street, by the sword. He was no trifle, no civil-rights lawyer, no ivory tower professor living comfortably in the suburbs. He was a sly-boots, crafty ...

"You sound like Earl Long," Fletcher said.

"Hear me out!" Born protested.

"Listen, friend. We've known each other a long time." Fletcher leaned across the table, his voice smooth and low now. "How much do you know? Have you really checked him out? Have you seen the FBI file? Do you remember a few years back, the syndicate guy who was killed in the barber's chair? Does your memory go back that far? Do you know who let that contract? Do you know ..."

"A smear, not proved!" Born shouted.

"Not according to J. Edgar," Fletcher said.

The case lost, Born decided to push ahead with what he truly felt. Metaphorically, he said—in metaphors, with so much whiteness directing the law of the land, why not a bit of blackness? A thousand utopians, one dystopian—or the reverse, depending on the angle of vision. Was it not true that the times were complex, crazed really? He saw in Maxey an energy and spirit denied to others, his insights hard won. In the area of the criminal law ...

"Oh, for Christ's sake," Fletcher exploded. He began to laugh; he threw his head back and the crash of laughter filled the silence of the room. Then he waved at a startled waiter and jiggled his fist, signaling for the check.

"He knows as much as the rest of them," Born went on, surprised that he had gone so far, surprised at his passion and his logic. "You put him on the court for the same reason that you put old Joe Kennedy on the SEC, same damned reason exactly!"

Fletcher shook his head, still smiling.

"He's a reformed man," Born said quietly.

"Sure."

"In a way, a lovely man."

"Right right right."

"An elegant man."

"Sure."

"There's precedent for this."

"Okay," Fletcher said. "Joke's over."

Then Born played his last card. "The president ..."

"Finish your drink, let's get out of here," Fletcher said.


II

In due course, Willard Maxey returned to Harlem, without a word of thanks or of farewell. One morning he was gone, checked out of the Hay Adams for good. Carney handled the billing (ignoring, and not informing Weiss, that client Maxey—his final sardonic comment—had sent a bill to *them*, "for services rendered"). The case was closed in the press. Technically, the hearings had been recessed, but everyone knew they would not be reopened.

The president announced that his old friend had decided to withdraw; the case slid off into limbo. Born, who had devoted so much energy to the defense of the judge, was dispirited and mortified by the outcome. Nothing settled, nothing solved; Maxey neither confirmed nor denied, neither innocent nor guilty, the case itself slipped out of sight—not the way it should be, though often was. Born knew this, but hated to accept it. The essential American condition, no resolution.

The night after the hearings ended for good, Born stayed late in his office with a bottle of Scotch and a bucket of ice, reviewing his professional life. Carney and Weiss had switched immediately to neglected business, accepting the change of pace without comment or complaint. Maxey was done; now it was time to get back to work, real work, not the aberration of a public hearing, something conducted in full view of press and public. Born was a man accustomed to workable solutions, guilt or innocence of some kind, by decision of judge, jury, commissioner, or mediator. An approach pursued, a period at the end of a sentence. But not limbo.

He had no desire to go home. No desire for his wife or for anything else. He sat at his desk and drank the whiskey and looked at the artifice of his lawyer's life, the yellow pads, the Parkers, the stationery, the picture of his wife on the bookshelf (it resembled the picture of the president on a post office wall).

Her face was half hidden behind a pile of printed matter, briefs, abstracts, law journals. Her face began at the nose, a good nose he thought; smallish, pert, inquiring. The eyes were good, too, large and luminous when not concealed behind horned-rims. The picture was five years old at least, and he noticed with regret that her hair was a deep brown; had been then. The photograph did not show the recent streaks of chemical gray. The papers hid her expression from him. Was she smiling: No, it was a straight-on look, a glance almost. He remembered taking the picture himself, on a Sunday picnic in Montrose Park.

The bottle was three-quarters done, the taste stuck in his throat. Born thought he'd go home. Where was that? A small flat on Q Street in Georgetown. A sparsely furnished flat, a flat with books. A flat less personal than his own office. He wished now that he'd stayed clear, away from the public-ness of it. The psychology, the cheating—memos for the press, old scores settled deftly, new ones accumulated. What was he doing making law for politicians? They made their own law anyway. He made it for the politicians; she made it for the State Department. That was the unhappy part, but he could not deny that he felt comfortable in his office, surrounded by his possessions. His cracked leather chair tilted back, his feet on the worn wooden desk.

Hypnotic, though: the front bench of witnesses, Fletcher and the committee chairman, and Carney's strong soft voice— a voice to silence turtles, that one. Hypnotic, stunning in timbre, Carney could silence turtles and charm angels. But he had no faith in Maxey—at the end Carney was just going through the motions; Maxey was one more client who had got his, one way or another, and would be defended ... as required. Gripped by an awful melancholy just then, Born poured the last of his bottle into the glass, and filled the glass with ice. A little of the whiskey spilled on the desk blotter, and he watched the stain spread. Maxey. He'd turned to Carney and Born on the last day and laughed out loud, a long braying haaaaaaaaaaaaaaaaaaa. And Carney had just looked at him with a frozen smile. "Ha-ha-ha," Carney said.

The whiskey was sour to his taste. Filled-up drunk now, he rummaged through his filing cabinet, looking for the black loose-leaf notebook from Boston. His accounts. He found it, filed under INVESTMENTS, and took it out, leaning unsteadily against the steel gray cabinet. The last report was a month old; it represented the latest advance. Each report was an advance on the last, a tribute to the abundance of the American economy and the foxy investment banker from Boston who handled all the money, his and hers. Well diversified, Born thought. Brilliantly, wonderfully diversified. Oils, furnaces, autos, textbooks, computer forms, photographic processes, textiles, and a bank in Brookline. The numbers danced and swam; he could not keep them straight. They would not add. He slumped against the file cabinet and the black notebook fell to the floor, the pages spilling. The room spun, and before he dropped to the couch he wished—it was a fleeting desire—that he had joined the government as he'd intended. He'd meant to embrace physics and law, something solid; a floor under his feet. He thought about his wife then, so sure in her instincts; so capable, so independent. He turned his head to see the white papers scattered on the floor. His investments. He drunkenly understood then that he'd made his life. It was his, no one else's.

· · ·

"In any event it wasn't your kind of case," his wife said to him a few nights later. "Never was. What do you care about it anyway? When he left he didn't even say thanks."

"He sent Carney a bill," Born said, then warned: "That's *entre nous*, between us."

"Well, there you are. Between us."

Born laughed: "… a bill for $6,000, a thou a week. I guess he figured he was doing us a favor, giving Carney and me a little post-graduate education. That's class," Born said.

"Life goes on."

"Six thou," Born mused. He did not tell his wife of the other transactions. These were facts he did not want her to have; he did not know what she'd make of them. "A thou a week."

His wife said nothing.

"I put myself into it," he said. He felt that he had withdrawn from an exhilarating war. There was no place to go now. He was astonished: they'd done all they could, and still they'd lost.

She talked about her job at the State Department. She'd spent the week researching legal contradictions in a proposal of the Joint Chiefs of Staff. These people are *incredible* she said. "They want another base … well, it's top secret," she said playfully. "Can't breathe a word."

Born smiled, distracted.

"Of course, if you'll read the morning paper …"

"Do you want another drink?"

She looked at him, surprised. Born rarely had more than two drinks before dinner.

"Do you?"

"Not me," she said. "I'm working tomorrow."

He made himself a Scotch and soda, and wandered into the

kitchen. A steak was defrosting on the counter; a dish of cottage cheese lay half-eaten in the sink. His wife stockpiled cottage cheese and steaks like the Army stockpiled weapons.

"Do you want to eat now?"

"No," he said. He was hollow, but not hungry. He saw her in the living room, her feet curled under her on the sofa. Her attaché case was on her knees; she was reading a document, underlining words in a red pencil as she went. He supposed it was the top secret document, the story in the newspapers that morning. He watched her concentrate on the words, a pencil between her teeth; he thought she looked very young. Outside, the light failed; it was dusk, a warm evening at the end of September, summer coming into fall. He finished his drink and walked into the bedroom and shed his business suit for a pair of workpants and a sweater.

She was still reading when he returned to the living room, and did not look up when he opened the front door.

"I'm going out for a walk," he said.

"Unh?" She looked up.

"Not long."

"You have a good walk."

Born saw that she did not remove her finger from the place she'd been reading. Her look was distracted; she was absorbed with a proposal of the Joint Chiefs of Staff. On the street he paused, uncertain which way to walk. In the old days there were friends within walking distance, but they'd all moved to the suburbs, with their children and station wagons; Georgetown was too expensive. He thought it was a strange town in which to live; now a dim and ghostly town, the inhabitants afraid to go forth in the dark.

He strolled down 30th Street to O, feeling furtive, alone in the street. Then he turned toward Wisconsin Avenue, the main stem. A police officer on a motor scooter slid past, slowed briefly, and went on. He looked at the houses and thought that Georgetown was perfectly preserved, a museum piece. Weiss's house loomed ahead of him; he paused on the sidewalk to look through the hedge. Lights were on in Weiss's study; he thought of the old man in his leather chair, reading Blackstone or Defoe or Saint-Simon, or whoever occupied his time now, after dark in the museum. He stood quietly for a moment, listening to the traffic on Wisconsin Avenue. Then he walked up the steps to Weiss's house and rang the bell.

The old man was cordial and asked him in. He offered cognac or a Scotch and soda. The light was on over the chair, a leather-bound book opened beside it. Born was apologetic and tried to leave; the room was so very private. He could see Weiss in the morning, at the office. No, Weiss said that he wanted to talk ...

Weiss showed Born his books; he was particularly pleased with his shelf of Mencken, including six years of *Smart Set*, bound. He'd known Mencken in the '30s and '40s, and they'd had an episodic correspondence, several examples of which were later published in the *Letters*. Once or twice a month they lunched together in Baltimore. Weiss smiled, and said that his friends were mostly gone now, Mencken only one of many. There were others, Felix Frankfurter, Dean Acheson; all dead. A sparrow among eagles, Weiss murmured. "I'm retiring at the end of the year," he said.

Born was astonished; he assumed that Weiss would stay on as long as there was an office for him. He could not imagine

the firm minus Weiss, or Weiss minus the law. He told him that
and the old man grunted, sad-eyed.

"You young fellows run the place now. With Carney." Born
lit a cigarette, destitute; he said nothing. "I didn't approve of
Maxey, not at all."

"We knew that," Born said. "Carney really didn't have any
choice."

Weiss looked at him a moment, then took a long draught of
his brandy and soda. "You liked him; I could never understand
why." He shook his head: "Not a quality man."

"Well, a different quality."

"Character's all one quality," Weiss said grimly. Then, suddenly: "You know we paid off."

Born nodded and raised his head, a question.

"Carney did. Never mind to whom. That's unimportant,
and doubly unimportant since we got nothing for the payoff.
Not one damned thing." Weiss leaned back, his hands gripping
his knees. "We blackbagged. *My* firm. No better than those
scoundrels in …" He named a law office in K street that spe-
cialized in political money, campaign contributions. "I think it's
the only time it ever happened. Oh, no one will ever know. It'll
never see the light of day, because there's a built-in protection
all around. No one will know. Except of course he who got
paid. He knows."

"Barkis is willin'," Born muttered. He looked away, to one
side, then back at Weiss, slumped in his chair, a drink in his
hand, the glass balanced on his belly.

"Scoundrels," Weiss said again. "We've never done dirty
work of that kind, never. We've counseled our clients in the
best way we knew how, right or wrong, innocent or guilty—or

WARD JUST

more likely a little of both. We've used the law any way we could, as advocates. That's what the common law is all about. You use the weapons at hand. We've protected our clients from the ... mindlessness of the bureaucrats and the interference of politicians or their own stupidity. But we've never blackbagged. We've never paid off. Anyone. No matter who asked us, we'd tell them to take it up with someone else."

Born drew back, watching the older man. He could not have been innocent of Carney's work. But perhaps he was, or chose to be. Carney seldom specified what he did, or how he did it. Carney occupied one half of the office, Weiss the other half. Weiss did not often inquire into the Carney half.

"Who got the bill for Maxey?" Born wondered how much Weiss knew.

The old man shrugged. "Carney took care of it."

"But who paid it?"

"I suppose the White House paid it; we billed them a flat fee of twenty thousand dollars. For all I know the president picked it up, like a restaurant check. How would I know? I know for dead sure that Willard Maxey never paid it; that charlatan never paid a bill in his life. That's the lesson of this administration, if you're interested in lessons. They're first-class aristocrats and second-class scoundrels. With the opposition, it's the other way around."

Born smiled; the old man had not lost his juice. But he was not well informed on the other matters. The bill had been 50, not 20. And it had been presented, by hand, to the president's personal attorney, who advised them that he had forwarded it "on." But Born was surprised that Weiss knew of the payoff; Carney must have been indiscreet—most uncharacteristic of him. The money, in the form of a campaign contribution, had gone to a senator on the committee in return for support. But all the senator delivered was neutrality. In the circumstances, Carney philosophically observed, it was better than nothing.

"What will you do now?" Born asked gently.

"Travel," Weiss said. "My indulgence, my passion, is antiquity. I propose to spend a year in Greece and Turkey and the islands. I've friends there. I may write a bit, of this and that."

They were silent then, listening to the ticking of the clock on the mantel. Born made a drink for himself and went to the window. The street was empty, the time near midnight. He wanted to explain his exhaustion to the old man, to receive assurances that his own vitality would return. Men hit troughs in their lives, inexplicable depressions. Early male menopause he thought, and smiled. His head was empty; the mine was worked dry. He wondered suddenly if he were impotent.

"How's your wife?" Weiss asked.

"Working hard." He spoke from the window without turning around. The truth was, he didn't know how she was; he'd hardly seen her for six weeks. "She likes her job; I know that much. She's at home now reading top-secret papers. She's all wrapped up in that, as I used to be in the brownstone." He moved away from the window to the fireplace.

Weiss's eyes were closed, and he'd put his drink back on the sideboard. Born looked around the room, then walked quietly to the door. He wondered if he should turn off the lights, but decided against that. He walked into the foyer and was stepping out the door when he heard the old man from the other room.

"When I got into a crack, I used to say the hell with it and get away for a week. Sometimes alone, sometimes not." Weiss laughed, a dry rustle. "Most often not, now that I think about it. Once or twice I found a young lady." Pause. "Once Mencken and I ..." Then he was silent, the sentence unfinished, and Born said goodnight to him and walked out the door.


Each day, from his window in the brownstone, he watched the progress of an office building across the street. A white sign, red lettering, announced it would contain a government commission. Robust workers in hardhats balanced themselves on steel girders, main beams defining the skeleton structure. The first month, Born marked the changes on a sheet of ledger paper: second stories becoming third and fourth, the girders lifted into place by cranes in the street. The men on the main beams caught the girders in midair, they seemed to hold them as effortlessly as weight lifters hoisting a feather. Men guided two-ton girders into place, fastening them, welding them one to the others. In the mornings he heard music from transistor radios perched high on the beams: modern music between two-minute news reports and commercial announcements.

The new building was identical to the one beside it; yellow facing (from his distance it had the look and texture of plastic) and severe rectangular windows, large black spaces out of which the civil servants could gaze. All of it was identical: the overhanging marquee at street level, a penthouse on top, the parking lot underneath. Under the marquee the government planted trees. There were three of them, scrawny in November; they were without leaves, there was no sign of life. The trees arrived one morning, their roots entombed in burlap;

there they sat for a week, untouched. Then they were put into the ground.

With mounting interest, Born watched the government commission move into its new offices. The inventory: metal desks, filing cabinets—a thousand filing cabinets, some of them secured with combination locks. The desks and filing cabinets were gray angled furniture, placed in equipoise in the offices, these spaces arranged with the precision of Japanese rock gardens, the desks just so under the windows, the filing cabinets on the south wall, pen sets and white tin staplers placed about like ceremonial satsuma. Born watched the procession from his window: the wastebaskets, carpets, rubber plants, water coolers, typewriters, leather chairs, odd wide sofas, typing tables, adding machines, conference tables (these coffin-shaped for easy listening), bookshelves, and finally boxes, hundreds of them, containing the paper—stationery, Xerox paper, requisition slips, petty cash forms, envelopes, graph paper, scratch paper. Three months from beginning to end—amazing how quickly they threw up buildings these days! Then the people came to work.

Born became fussy and quarrelsome in his early middle age. He was stale, his vitality flagged, and he now quit the office every day at 6. Sometimes he carried a briefcase of work, more often not. He'd return to the apartment in Georgetown and spend a silent evening with his wife, if she were home, or with the television set, if she were not. His colleagues remarked on the change, saying nothing to him directly for the first six months. Born, who had worked harder than anyone else in the office for ten years, was entitled to his lapse. But the partners (there were now nine of them) no longer wanted him in on their important cases; his presence was depressing, bad for business. Carney ignored him entirely; Born's only contact was with Weiss, who maintained office hours even after his early retirement; he planned to move to Greece in June.

It was Weiss, finally, who was urged to talk with him. Get Born out of town, get him on holiday. Convince him to take six months' leave, salary to continue. His position was secure.

"They think you ought to take a vacation," Weiss told him one morning.

"Do clients approve of suntans?" Born was watching a bureaucrat dictate to his secretary in an office opposite his, across the street in the government building. The secretary sat primly; the bureaucrat circled in front of the desk.

"You're off your pace," Weiss said. "You need a change. It's no disgrace. We all get tired from time to time. Batteries run down." This was a familiar speech; Weiss knew it by heart. "Take a vacation; my God you've only had—how many—three or four since you've been here. Your wife would be willing to do that, I'm sure." When Born did not reply, Weiss added quietly: "I'll be glad to talk with her, if you'd like."

"She's wrapped up in her job," he said.

"Well, unwrap her."

Born smiled.

Weiss probed: "Are you sure? Women ..." he began.

"One thing and another," Born said.

Weiss wanted to tell Born about his wife, the bright girl he'd met—seen—only half a dozen times in the ten years Born had worked for him. He suspected more than he knew, but Weiss liked to think that his instincts were sound.

"Have you talked to her about it?"

Born shook his head. He felt weary, wrung out.

"Look, it might be better between you if you took the holi-day. Alone, if need be. If it's a question of money, the firm ..." Weiss's voice trailed off.

"No, it's not money," Born said, laughing and shaking his head. The idea of a loan seemed to amuse him. "No, as a mat-ter of fact I guess my wife and I have many thousands ... salted away. I'd guess we have close to a quarter of a million dollars in securities, maybe more."

Weiss scowled; he wondered if it were possible. Then he remembered the apartment in Georgetown, sparsely fur-nished. They had no children, no family commitments of any kind. They had few expensive tastes. He guessed that it was possible after all.

"I've done well in the market," Born said. "I go in and stay in; the best stocks are like the best clubs. So I never get caught or stuck in any way." He smiled wanly. "If you don't spend it, it piles up. Spontaneous generation. Q.E.D. Isn't that something? A quarter of a million. Maybe more."

"Well," Weiss said. Then, dryly: "It's a conversation stopper all right."

"It's all there, and I don't spend it."

"Well, that's the point."

"All this damned money." Born grinned.

Weiss was confused; there was nothing he could say. Born was staring serenely into the middle distance, a bleak smile on his face.

"Isn't it ironic as hell?"

"I suppose," Weiss said. That was what Born apparently wanted, money, and that's what he had now. Many people had less.

"It'll pass," Born said. "I need some more time, just a bit."

"They're worried ..."

"There's nothing to worry about. Tell them that."

"I do want to assure you of the good will of everyone here," Weiss said softly, almost tenderly.

Born stared across the desk at him, tears in his eyes. Just then he wanted to trust the old man, to confide everything in him, to become his brother. But he did not know what it was that he wanted to say. He could not find the words, or any words that Weiss would understand. He knew only that something was dead inside him—ambition, other desires. He knew that in atomic physics the laws of cause and effect yield finally to the laws of chance, a game of craps. The measurement of motion depended on the position of the observer, and the instruments used. More: approaching the speed of light, objects changed their shape, highly sensitive instruments produced highly complex definitions ... of the laws of chance. He'd quit theoretical physics for practical law, a question for an answer. But it hadn't worked out. The moving body had gone beyond measurement: Born's special theory of relativity.

Weiss had turned away, flustered. "They're concerned."

"A question of distance," Born said.

Weiss looked at him, puzzled.

"It makes no sense," Born said.

"What?"

"This law. It's barren as hell, isn't it?" He thought of Weiss and his amateur archaeology. Devotion to the law became, with the necessary transpositions, devotion to antiquity. Lucky Weiss. "My life," he said, "it's here."

"Of course," Weiss said. He was comfortable now, he understood. "You've a place here."

"Yes," Born said.

Weiss was impatient: "Then pull out of whatever it is that you're in. Good God, life goes on. I don't know what it is; I know it couldn't be Maxey. You've got to understand that Maxey isn't important, it's just a *case*. Like any other. Is it your wife?" He paused, forgetting himself a moment: he peered at Born across the cluttered desk. "That doesn't matter, either. Get a hold of yourself. These other things, they're gone and forgotten."

Born muttered something; Weiss didn't hear what it was.

"Right. So you've got to pull up your socks. Do something outrageous." Weiss smiled and leaned back in the chair. "Forget the job. Go buy a damned expensive car. Or a diamond for your wife. Buy both, with all that money. I thought you said you didn't care for money."

"Did," Born said.

"Well, all right."

Born nodded. Exactly.

"You can't take it with you."

"I wouldn't want to do it anyway."

Weiss lit a cigarette, looking at Born through the smoke. A light on Born's telephone winked, and the younger man picked up the receiver and began to talk. Weiss thought it sounded like a long conversation, so he got up to leave. Born spun in his chair, running a hand through his hair. Weiss stood for a moment, listening to the telephone conversation. The details of a widow's trust, how much for this grandchild, how much for that. The principal available—when? At what age does competence commence? Thirty years? Or not at all! A perpetual trust! The money withheld forever! Inviolate! Widows, Weiss thought with a smile. This would be a very long conversation. Born was listening to the widow and smiling wryly at Weiss. Weiss closed the door and left Born to it.

Attenuated, the trees without leaves reached to the roof of the apartment house. The sun lowered behind the red brick. Varying his route, walking slowly up O Street, Born heard voices behind the houses: cocktail parties in progress in backyard gardens; the sound of laughter and music filled the street. This was the first warm night of the season, a glowing April dusk. He took off his jacket and strolled uphill, listening to cocktail noise, furious laughter.

He let himself in; she was not at home. He put his empty briefcase on the table and leafed through the mail: two embassy receptions and a half dozen letters from friends, scattered now around the country. They were part of another life, well-lived. He went to fetch ice and glasses. He emptied the ice into a bucket and put the bucket on the drinks tray. Next to the bucket went the gin and the Schweppes. Absently, he put two glasses on the tray. Then he reflected that it was a foolish ritual: why not make drinks in the kitchen and avoid the mess. There was only himself and conceivably her, if she arrived home in time. However, he lifted the drinks tray and conveyed it into the living room. The air conditioner was silent; the room hot. He opened the window and stood before it a moment, watching the street. Distracted by the crossbars in the windows, he closed his eyes. He hoped to see her in a taxicab, to watch her alight, pay the driver, and hurry, so jaunty now, across the sidewalk and into the apartment house. But the street was empty of cabs, or women with briefcases. He turned away from the window to the room. Preparing his drink, he attended the evening news. The television bubbled into life. The war, the children, the blacks, the president, the economy, the Russians, the market, the weather. The news done, Born made himself another drink and thought, however briefly, about his life.

### III

When he returned from two weeks in Nassau, Born found the inevitable note. His wife had moved out, and taken an apartment in the same building, one floor below. The note explained that she could not resist the move, once she knew that the apartment was available. She needed more time to herself, for her work and her private life, and the various efforts she made. He was happier alone anyway. The note read, in part:

It'll be better for us. I have my books and my other things. I've taken my files, and the law books that are mine. Steaks are in the freezer.

Indulge an old man; I was stunned by that last sentence. I think I have never read words so sorrowful, or so bleak. Born accepted the note as unavoidable, I think even with a sense of relief. The world closed in around him. At any event, he told me a little later, they saw each other on weekends and occasionally she'd bring a legal problem to him for comment. Once or twice, staring at their street from the window, he saw her enter the building with a man, their arms laden with groceries, both of them clutching briefcases.

Whether for that or for other reasons, we at the office witnessed an extraordinary transformation. Born appeared to age before our eyes, becoming heavier and acquiring a gravity of manner that was alarming in so young a man. His hair turned gray, and he seemed to move with effort. His voice deepened and became dull; he settled.

About the time Born returned from the Caribbean, Carney suffered his stroke and the firm was plunged into another period of turmoil. To put it mildly, Carney ran a closed shop and it was never entirely clear to any of us precisely how he handled his assignments. But he had a number of projects on his calendar, and these were spread among the senior men in the office. I came out of retirement, and postponed my journey abroad, to supervise the distribution and to reassure our older clients. Carney was in an oxygen tent, and in no position to advise us on anything.

Born accepted his share without complaint, although the rest of us were worried that he was not up to it. I mean by that his demeanor, which had become quite ponderous. A lawyer needs a light touch: not always and not often, but when it is useful it is very useful. But in the event we were proved wrong. Working more slowly than before, Born nevertheless dealt with Carney's cases quite satisfactorily. However, he did not join in the office jokes, the speculation about who would inherit the membership in Burning Tree, the mystery of the disappearance of Carney's diary and private telephone book, and (I must say, even I was amused) the abrupt departure of three clients. We never learned what their business was, nor Carney's part in it. We simply received registered letters that they were "canceling," due to the indisposition of their friend and counselor.

I saw Born much less frequently than before, owing to my own preoccupation with clients. When a senior partner leaves a small firm, it is always very difficult to assure clients that nothing has changed; Carney's commanding personality, and astonishingly varied contacts in the Washington political world, made it doubly difficult. There were rumors everywhere, and it fell to the rest of us to make it absolutely clear that our ship was in shape and on course. This we did, I am proud to say, and Born deserves much of the credit. He took four of Carney's most setaceous cases, and dealt with them subtly and with no pomp; he even seemed to enjoy it, and in the light of subsequent events, his tenacity was all the more admirable.

One night toward the end of the Carney crisis, I left the office late. I searched for a cab in vain, then decided I would walk home. One needed to think, and the hour's walk would do me good. I thought that once I was in Georgetown, I would dine out.

I was crossing Dupont Circle, avoiding the crowds, when I heard my name, and turned round to see a young woman hurrying toward me. I did not recognize her at first, then saw it was Born's wife. I was not especially pleased to see her. Her husband was my friend and colleague, and while theirs was not a situation where it was necessary (or even advisable) to take sides, I nevertheless *did* take sides. I didn't like her one bit.

She asked me if I was walking to Georgetown, and I said that I was. To my surprise, she hooked her arm through mine and said she'd walk with me as far as P Street. She explained that she was meeting Born at Martin's Tavern for a late dinner.

"How is he?" she asked.

"He's just fine," I replied. I thought I would go further; I wanted her to get the message that he was very fine indeed. "He's been absolutely invaluable the past few weeks. The vacation did him a lot of good," I said.

She nodded and we walked on a little.

"Hasn't he aged," she said. It was not a question but a statement, and seemed to contain some sympathy—or interest anyway.

"He's heavier, older ..."

"I don't mean that. I mean his personality. The way he thinks. It seemed to happen overnight."

"It happened when you moved out," I said.

"No, it's convenient to think so, but it's not true. It began before that. It began last summer, after the Maxey ... interlude. He was impotent, you know. But often the most obvious things are not the most important things, *n'est-ce pas*? Before he went away, he started reading his physics books again. You know that he started out in college wanting to be a scientist. It didn't last long; the law overcame physics when he was about twenty. But he was very good at it, straight A's his first two years at Stanford. Kudos, a bright and limitless future. His professors thought that he had a future in theoretical physics. No, I think he lost his logic somewhere. Either he did or the law did, one or the other ..." she talked on, as casually as if Born were a distant relative or a colleague at the office. There was nothing I could say to her, so I kept quiet. "Lost logic," she said again.

"What exactly does that mean, 'Lost his logic?'"

"I wish I knew. It's his phrase, not mine."

"Well, I think it's simpler to say that he went through a bad period. Most people do, sometime in their lives."

"He's not through it yet. And Nassau didn't help any. It was a dumb choice."

"Yes," I admitted.

"You might ask Carney about the other thing."

"Carney?"

"Did Carney like him?"

"Respect would be a better word," I said.

"I think he was afraid of Carney, a little." She looked at me and smiled, a smile both dazzling and wicked.

"That makes no sense to me," I said.

"I didn't think it would," she replied, and when I turned to her, angry at the implication, she smiled again. "I mean it's probably nonsense. It probably isn't true."

"Your husband is not a man to be pushed this way and that. Maxey was a surprise to him, I'll grant that. But Carney and I, we're not sorcerers. Your husband was one of several younger partners; he wasn't singled out in any way. He was with us on the Maxey case because he knew Fletcher and was qualified in other ways. Your husband took that case far too seriously; it's a cardinal sin in a lawyer."

"Born is very complicated," she said.

We walked on in silence. The traffic was abnormally heavy,

and the exhaust fumes had us both coughing. My fists, closed around two briefcases, were sweating. It is a lawyer's habit to pose blunt questions, from nowhere, with no warning. It often throws a witness off balance; a pause or a silence can give a lawyer clues to the truth, to things otherwise concealed. "Born told me once that you'd both made a lot of money," I said. "He told me that you had a quarter of a million dollars. 'Salted away,' I believe the phrase was."

"More than that," she said quickly. "My guess would be, it's closer to three hundred thousand now. It's managed by one of those chi-chi investment bankers in Boston. It just grows and grows and grows; it's watched very carefully. My husband is good with money, always has been. He's excellent with numbers," she said, grinning suddenly.

"Why?"

"The money? I'm not sure, really. It goes way back, to the time before we were married. We used to laugh a lot about money. At one time he thought he needed money to work for the government. He found out he didn't, really, and then he found out he liked the law. But the money was there, and it remained a kind of goal for him. I guess that was it, although he never talked about it much."

"But not for you."

"No, not for me. Money never meant anything to me."

"Why not?"

"Well, that was *his* thing, wasn't it? I found out very early that you don't mix lives. I mean by that, mix careers. Everything in its place. I was very lucky to learn it early. Born was less lucky. It messes up your mind, *n'est ce pas?*"

"*N'est-ce pas*," I said, with as much sarcasm as I could muster.

"It's too bad we can't be friends," she said.

"We could be," I said. "But we're on different sides of the fence." I was anxious to get away from her, to go home and drink a cocktail. I wanted to be done with it. "There's your husband now, up ahead." Born was standing on the corner of 31st and P. He looked portly and prosperous, and was consulting his watch as we approached.

She stepped in front of me then, her back to her husband, and addressed me in an undertone, passionate and direct and utterly remorseless. "You can never know what's going on in people's lives, Mr. Weiss. The outside is not the inside; most lawyers know that. You can take all the facts and incidents and add them up, inventory them like a shoe clerk and all you have, still, is just that ... an inventory. My husband and I lived—live— the way we do, why? Look at him on the sidewalk, fat and solemn, sad, complacent, serious, and what does that mean? We've lived the way we could, the way we had to. There wasn't any other way, or any way that we could see, once we'd chosen our ... professions. Lived in the time and place that we did. In law school he was excellent, a mutual friend told me that. My husband was excellent at mock court, either as prosecutor or as defense counsel. Either way, it made no difference to him, offense or defense, the sum was the same. The professor who supervised the mock court once said that Born was hard to hit. He meant elusive, but more than elusive he meant fast and variable. A man in motion. You were quite right to say that he took the Maxey case too seriously; you with your wonderful insight. Your intelligence. Your imagination. Your compassion. Your ethics. You hit a bull's eye. But that's in the past tense now, isn't it? Isn't it just that, Mr. Weiss?"

She left me without another word and walked to the corner to collect Born. I watched her go, a trim young woman, walking swiftly, stepping straight to her husband, kissing him on the cheek—indifferently, lightly, no affection there I thought—and taking his arm to march across 31st Street and move on down to Martin's Tavern.

The thing was meticulously done, directly in character. Born wanted a will drawn, and he wanted me to draw it. I have never seen a lawyer, and I have watched hundreds, so attentive to details. We went over every line in the document, sometimes twice and three times even after the thing had been written, signed, and witnessed. We analyzed every trust mechanism, every tax shelter, every legal device by which a rich man can hide his money. Some of these he accepted, some he rejected—he said he wanted an airtight will that would stand every test, a will that no challenge could break. It was not a complicated document; Born divided his money along traditional lines. I did not advise him on the distribution of income, because of course I was biased. I wanted her cut off at the legal minimum. In the event, he cared more about the precision of the language than the practical effect. When we were finished it was a model testament, the more so for being quite straightforward.

I saw nothing amiss; if anything Born was more cheerful than usual the night we finished the will and put it away in the office safe. He suggested a nightcap and we sat in my office and opened the whiskey bottle.

"Did you enjoy talking to my wife the other night?"

I thought I saw a gleam of humor in his eyes, but I answered soberly: "We talked for some time."

"That's what she said, and that wasn't what I asked. I asked if you enjoyed it."

"Not particularly."

He dug the palms of his hands into his eyes, the gesture of a wary, weary man. But his voice was clear and sharp. "She's doing very well at the Department. She's carved out quite a career for herself. It shows you what legal training can accomplish."

I listened for sarcasm, heard none, and let Born continue.

"I don't think she really knows much or cares about foreign affairs. But she's a determined woman."

"Lawyers and diplomats," I said. "We honor the same devils."

"Well, she enjoyed talking to you anyway."

"That's what she said?"

"More or less."

"I don't pretend to understand your wife." He looked up then and smiled broadly. "Do you think," I asked. "Do you think she's *happy*?"

Born gave me a special look, one he reserved for people who asked him obtuse questions. I was sorry I'd said anything, but the woman irritated me beyond all bounds. I didn't understand how he could put up with her. However, I waited for an answer.

"I don't know," Born said. He put more ice cubes and whiskey in our glasses, and we were both silent for a moment. "There was a time when we understood each other perfectly; it was a sort of ESP. I'm out of practice for that now; we don't see each other very often. But we're still connected in a strange

way, I'm certain of that. We're still married. I think she understands the thing better than I do." He paused, obviously distracted. "I could tell that she liked you very much. That much
was obvious to me."

I said nothing to that; it was completely untrue. I thought he
was wrong about the other as well. Then we talked of office
matters and finished our drinks and prepared to leave. Born
turned to me in the elevator, a grim expression on his face.

"Is Carney really returning?"

I was surprised at the question; I thought I was the only one
who knew. "Only part time," I said. "It's what they call work
therapy, that as much as anything else. He wants to ride in the
elevator and sit in his own office again. Poor chap, he can't
walk at all and is still quite confused. It'll only be for an hour or
so a day."

"But he won't be practicing."

"No. He'll never practice again. This is just a way to make
him feel better; feel a part of the firm again." I found myself
saying these words to reassure Born.

"What do you know about that," Born said.

We left the brownstone and that was the last time I saw him.
His movements from that hour can only be surmised. It
appears that he walked home and had several drinks, and the
next morning took a cab to Dulles, and there boarded a plane
for Nassau. He checked into a small hotel that night, signing
the guest register in bold, distinct script; he listed the brownstone as his address. He asked the manager to take his passport
and an attaché case he was carrying, and put them into the
hotel safe. The manager obliged, and Born returned to his
room for the evening. He was found a day later on a deserted

beach, away from the city; the official verdict was death by drowning. Suicide is an ugly word in resorts. Born's was an inconspicuous death, and the authorities found no note.

Why Nassau? There was no satisfactory answer to that; indeed no answer at all except the one confidently advanced by his wife. He'd mentioned the facts to her before, in another connection, as a legal curiosity. It had to do with taxes, death duties. He'd moved his stocks and bonds from Boston to a bank in Nassau; the attaché case contained cash and the only copies of his will. There were obvious legal advantages and no question at all of the basic logic: everything in Nassau was less demanding than the District of Columbia.


I am seated in the shadows. A bright July sun spills through the windows, painting the front benches a livid orange. The church is cool, the air soft, the heat has yet to work its way inside the building. A sweet southern day in summer, no day to bury the dead.

We are silent, listening to the musician out of sight in the balcony. I am no connoisseur of jazz music, so I do not know his name, but I am told that he is one of the great musicians in America, who for private reasons lives in Washington. He caresses the guitar slowly and beautifully; it is classical guitar, but the music is modern. The rich chords fall lightly; I imagine them sliding down the shaft of sunlight, filling the church.

This is a memorial service, and the widow is seated near the altar, front bench, friends on either side. Her head is bowed; her long dark hair reaches almost to the small of her back. We listen to the music for a quarter of an hour, and then I rise and move to the front of the church. I begin slowly, for I am undecided what it is that I want to say. My fingers tremble, and I lean against a pew to steady myself. I look over the heads of those in the church, and begin to speak. My voice is unfamiliar, harsh and metallic in the softness of the room.

"... our good friend," I begin.

Pause. The widow raises her head, inquiring; a look of encouragement; I see her at the edges of my vision.

"... a good man, a short life, a life full of promise. A distinguished attorney. A modern man."

Weak words; what else to say? There is more to Born than that. I hesitate and look at my feet. The silence surrounds me. I notice that Carney and his wheelchair are gone. The next words are lost, I speak them so swiftly. I sense them straining to hear. The widow has bent her head again, and I can see her shoulders shaking. The music has stopped, but now it begins again. The sunlight, soft chords.

"A man of his time."

I look at Born's wife; her head is in shadows. In the long silence that follows, she slowly turns toward me. Her lips frame a word, and I look at her closely to discover what it is. I cannot make it out, and she shrugs and smiles bleakly and bows her head again. I mean to end my eulogy: "A serious man." But I cannot complete the sentence, and walk slowly down the center aisle to my bench. I wanted to say that Born reminded me of an undefended fortress. And I wanted to speak again of tenacity, and pursuit and complexity. And devotion. But those were not observations that I cared to make in public, not to the widow.

PublicAffairs is a new publishing house and a tribute to the standards, values, and flair of three persons who have served as mentors to countless reporters, writers, editors, and book people of all kinds, including me.

I.F. STONE, proprietor of *I. F. Stone's Weekly*, combined a commitment to the First Amendment with entrepreneurial zeal and reporting skill and became one of the great independent journalists in American history. At the age of eighty, Izzy published *The Trial of Socrates*, which was a national bestseller. He wrote the book after he taught himself ancient Greek.

BENJAMIN C. BRADLEE was for nearly thirty years the charismatic editorial leader of *The Washington Post*. It was Ben who gave the *Post* the range and courage to pursue such historic issues as Watergate. He supported his reporters with a tenacity that made them fearless and it is no accident that so many became authors of influential, bestselling books.

ROBERT L. BERNSTEIN, the chief executive of Random House for more than a quarter century, guided one of the nation's premier publishing houses. Bob was personally responsible for many books of political dissent and argument that challenged tyranny around the globe. He is also the founder and longtime chair of Human Rights Watch, one of the most respected human rights organizations in the world.

———

For fifty years, the banner of Public Affairs Press was carried by its owner Morris B. Schnapper, who published Gandhi, Nasser, Toynbee, Truman and about 1,500 other authors. In 1983, Schnapper was described by *The Washington Post* as "a redoubtable gadfly." His legacy will endure in the books to come.

Peter Osnos, *Publisher*